the
planeless

Book One of The First Plane Trilogy

patti larsen

ALSO BY
PATTI LARSEN

The Hayle Coven Universe

The Hunted Series
Fiona Fleming Cozy Mysteries
The Nightshade Cases
The Clone Chronicles
The Diamond City Trilogy
Didi and the Gunslinger

and much, much more.
Find your new favorite author at
pattilarsen.com
Sign up for new releases
bit.ly/pattilarsenemail

chapter one

My lips smiled as the strains of "Happy Birthday" filled the living room of Syd's house. I think I did a decent job showing enthusiasm when the song wrapped up and everyone clapped while staring at me with their great expectations written all over their faces.

No one seemed to notice my discomfort or the fact my mouth trembled a little. Four years on Demonicon as Ruler had given me enough presence I suppose I was able to hide from the very people who made my anxiety worse. Not because I didn't love them. But because I did.

Perhaps I shouldn't have been surprised to find it was easier to pretend around those who hated me and watched my every move for failure, weakness or the merest flash of hesitation. Court and the nobles who pushed my limits every day had honed my ability. But sitting here in Syd's house—the house that used to be my home—stirred so many emotions I could hardly stand to be there, my human-appearing hands gripping the edge of the couch cushion beneath me so tightly I felt them cramp.

"Happy eighteenth, sweetheart." Mom leaned toward me from where she perched on the arm of the sofa, the ever-familiar floral touch of lilac making things worse. I hugged her quickly, knowing my embrace came across stiff, but unable to relax for fear I would weep all over my poor mother. She worried about me enough as it was. I saw it in her own trembling smile as she pulled away. It wasn't her fault I'd taken on a larger role than I likely should have at the tender age of fourteen. I wished I could assure her of that. I'd wanted my present position, craved it like the nectar that once possessed me. And when I looked up and into blue eyes watching me from across the room, I allowed the demon of jealousy living inside to surface and admit just why I pursued the First Seat of Demonicon so eagerly.

My beautiful older sister stood with one shoulder leaning against the entry, her long, almost black hair in a casual ponytail. Thick waves of it hung over her opposite shoulder, the ends curling upward around the curve of her chest. A plain blue t-shirt fitted perfectly over her flat stomach, skimming the waistband of her beat-up jeans. Sydlynn Hayle, coven leader and all-powerful maji, wore a pentagram necklace hung at the "V" of her neckline, sparkling in the light of the sun coming through the living room window. She looked so perfect standing there, casual, un-self-conscious, the burning envy I carried sizzled and popped to anxious life.

Syd cocked her head to one side, waves bouncing, eyebrows coming together. I felt her power reach for me and immediately blocked her, jerking my gaze from hers before she could force the issue.

I loved my sister with all my heart, but there were times like these when I hated her, too. I tried very hard not to allow the reality of being Syd's little sister weigh on me, but it was so difficult when my entire life was about scrutiny, either from those who couldn't wait for me to screw up, or from my family who watched with barely-concealed concern. Everyone waited for me to crack under the pressure.

The next person who compared anything I accomplished to what Syd would have done was going to perish in flame and agony.

Gabriel perched next to me, my sweet nephew eagerly watching my human fingers fumble over shiny paper, uncoiling carefully tied bows and ribbon as my heart lay dull and apathetic in my chest. Even his smiling face, sparkling hazel eyes and sweet spirit did nothing to make me feel better today. It shouldn't have been like this, the hollow feeling, the sense of distance from the very people I craved almost every day. But seeing them smile at each other, laugh easily as though they had no cares or considerations, just drove home the truth to me with every single outburst of mirth.

I was alone.

If you're done feeling sorry for yourself, my demon grandmother's mental voice grated over my mind, *let's finish up here and go home. You have work to do.*

Not so alone, after all. But having Ahbi Sanghamitra's spirit living inside me didn't exactly make the pressures of who I'd become any easier. If anything, the very dead former Ruler of Demonicon in my head at all times, poking and prodding, judging my every decision, only made things more difficult. I tried not to resent her, knowing she didn't ask for this existence, meeting a gristly end at the hands of Syd's nemesis, Ameline Benoit. And yet, there were many times I had to clench my teeth to keep from asking Ahbi to just leave already.

I could easily have blamed her for ruining my birthday moment. But I'd done that for myself. The cake tasted of ash in my mouth, the well-wishes as empty as my soul. I allowed the hug from Charlotte, the were bodyguard-turned-princess of her own people. Her blonde hair tickled my cheek as she released me. Gram was harder. No longer the old lady I grew up with, instead revitalized and renewed by the sorcery she claimed after giving up her witch magic, she nevertheless still had the ability to see through me with her piercing blue eyes. I loved her, always had, but didn't share the close bond she'd always had with Syd. So when she looked at me the way she did, it felt less like concern and more like she was judging me, weighing my worthiness against her favorite granddaughter.

Demetrius was different, at least. The diminutive sorcerer, his cherub face soft and smiling, kissed my cheek with enthusiasm before stepping back. I turned to hug my brother-in-law, the scent of chocolate and the touch of spicy magic traveling between us as Quaid kissed the top of my head.

"Sissy," he whispered. "Miss you."

I could have stood there in his arms for much longer, but doing so meant pushing the limit of tear control and I just couldn't have a breakdown here and now in front of the people I loved—and hated—the most.

Little three-year-old Ethie's soft, black curls brushed past my cheek as I lifted her into my arms. Bright blue eyes, the picture of her mother's, gazed at me with much more maturity than should have been available to a little girl.

"Meira," she said, tiny hands holding my face between them. "You 'kay?"

Almost undone by a serious toddler with a soul older than mine. I swallowed hard, kissing her before handing her with some haste to her father. I simply couldn't bring myself to release my control.

Sassafras watched me from the corner of the couch, amber eyes burning, though he didn't once say a word to me. It hurt, his silence. Of everyone here, he was the one I had been able to turn to in times of crisis. But no, not here and now. Allowing him in would mean a catastrophic meltdown, the exact thing I refused to show the people around me.

Dad was the hardest. My resentment burned against him as I turned to accept his hug. Resentment growing worse by the day as I dealt with the mess he'd left behind. His stint as Ruler might have been brief, but he succeeded in creating a singular hell I now lived and thanked him for with great sarcasm when I wasn't cursing him for his ideals.

He held me at arm's length as the family dispersed, frowning despite the small smile trying to lift his lips. He appeared as handsome as ever, though his demon form of red-tinted skin and curving black horns was long gone, perished with the destruction of his effigy. The diamond ring Syd forged from the shattered remains caught the sunlight and threw a stabbing ray into my eyes. I flinched, from more than the brightness, pulling free of him as my anger bubbled.

Ahbi wasn't much help. I'd stopped thinking of her as my grandmother, unable to keep the emotional connection between the two of us so simple since she insisted on trying to run my life. I understood Syd's more detached mode of address, though I would never admit it to her. It wasn't Syd who was the issue, it really wasn't, I knew so. But it was hard not to target my perfect sister who could do no wrong, the savior of everyone in the Universe when my life was falling apart.

"How are things at home?" Dad's rumbling voice offended me as much as the question. He didn't get to ask me such things. But instead of lashing out at him as I longed to, I drew a breath and faked a bright smile I knew did nothing to mask my anger.

"Just great," I said, the brittle edge to my voice cutting through me as Ahbi grumbled her dissatisfaction. If it were up to her, I would have given him an earful. But he was my father, and I loved him no matter what his plans for Demonicon had devolved into. And, at this point, yelling at him, throwing a tantrum, would do me little good. The damage was complete and Dad could do nothing to repair it. Not now he'd abandoned Demonicon for this plane and left me to wade into deep water without a lifejacket.

Us, Ahbi grumbled in my head. *You keep forgetting you're not the only one in this equation.*

I took a step back from Dad, smile cracking as she interfered.

If you don't mind, I shot back to her.

More grumbling echoed as Mom joined Dad. She was an entirely different story and, as she moved forward to

7

hug me again, I had to backpedal quickly to avoid her, my shoulders hitting Quaid square in the chest. He caught me, kept me level, let me go, all in silence. Mom, meanwhile, watched me with growing sadness as I rubbed my upper arms where my brother-in-law had gripped me. I needed to wipe away his empathy before it cracked me further.

"Thanks for the party." My smile returned, just as fake as before, but present, at least.

"We see so little of you these days, sweetheart," Mom said even as her hand slipped into Dad's. I saw them squeeze, felt my anger stir all over again. They had each other. I should have been happy for them instead of gripped by this irrational fury.

"A Ruler's work is never done." The joke came out easily, practiced and polished to a sheen from four years—longer, even—of needing to show the world I could handle it. That I was, in fact, just as good as my sister.

Speaking of whom, Syd joined our parents, frowning again, Quaid leaving me to join her. Gram and Demetrius, their youthful faces also drawn into concern, hovered behind.

I couldn't stand it. They would break me at any moment and I would finally confess what I feared was the truth. I'd made a terrible mistake. The role of Ruler was too big for me, far too vast, devouring me every moment, every breath until I could no longer take in air. That without Ahbi inside me I would have broken long ago, fled for home in disgrace.

How long had I stood on the sidelines while Syd saved the world? She'd suffered through hating her magic in her teens to grow into one of the most powerful magic users on this plane. Could I be the weak, fragile, helpless sister I believed I was and retreat, return to my family and be mediocre?

Ahbi snorted in my head. *Quit, then*, she sent.

I had to blink several times, use magic at last, to keep myself from bursting into tears. Blame and anger and guilt raced around inside me, a monster as huge as the one I carried in demon form, though this one demanded I break and let it out to expel all the pent-up emotion I suppressed.

"You know if you ever need anything…" Syd's frown deepened. Did she sense what I was feeling? Or was she just being her normal meddling self?

"Thank you," I said, the words emerging cold and crisp, "same to you."

I retrieved the two overflowing gift bags from the floor, heading for the hall and the kitchen without another word, and my family let me go. When had I become so irrational, so burdened by this bitterness refusing to release me? I heard her footsteps behind me as I descended into the basement to return home and part of me was glad.

While the rest of me wished Syd would just leave me alone.

The pentagram etched into the middle of the floor beckoned. I spun in place in the center of it, feeling the family magic of the Hayle coven caress me sadly, though I'd given up my connection to it long ago. One last layer of regret.

Time to go. I reached for the veil between planes, feeling the stretchy, slick surface answer my call even as Syd's power did the same. Impulse and anger moved me to block her, Ahbi responding with the same arrogance and my sister backed off.

"Meems, something is wrong. I know it." Syd didn't move, remaining on the edge of the pentagram etched onto the floor. "It's been getting worse the last year or so." She noticed, how incredible. I thought she only cared about herself and her own problems. I kicked myself mentally, furious at how unfair I was being, but unable to stop my bitterness. Syd's shoulders sagged forward as she brushed her hair back from her face. "I know you can handle whatever it is and that it's none of my business. I've always believed in you and I believe in you now. You were raised by the same mother I was." My sister's lip twisted in a half-smile. "You're a Hayle, no matter your status now. And Hayles are made for power." Her wry grin faded. "But we all need help sometimes. All of us. I just wanted you to know I'm here for you, no questions asked. Always."

Hate and tears and the need to lash out at her while I hugged her and cried on her shoulder warred in my soul.

"I have to go." How I managed to speak, I have no idea. The veil responded to my hasty jerk, tearing wide, the red-tinted gold light of Demonicon calling me back. For the barest instant, I felt my throat tighten, my stomach clench. I didn't want to go. How easy would it be to run back upstairs, to my old room, bury my head under the covers and just be Meira again?

But my room wasn't mine anymore. Syd's coven second, Sashenka Hensley, claimed it long ago. Nor was I Meems, Syd's little sister.

No, Ahbi sent with heat and frustration. *You are Senne Hathenemeira, Ruler of Demonicon. Exactly who you wanted to be.*

It didn't help my grandmother was right.

While Syd's power reached for me again, I crossed over, sealing the gap behind me.

Chapter Two

The tall, impeccably dressed figure of my aide stood waiting for me in my quarters. Pagomaris came to my side the moment I appeared, a constant in my life I wished at times would just go away and leave me alone. She was a reminder of my position, of how important it was I present a specific face and polish to the residents of Demonicon. Seeing her tightened the tension fist further.

A huge breath sat trapped in my chest as everything solidified, going rigid in anticipation. She smiled, her natural state, though her hands wrung before me as my demon form reverted from human to my taller, more muscular self.

"Ruler," she bowed to me, gesturing for her helpers to come forward. "We don't have much time."

There would be no use in grumbling. I'd learned long ago while she came across as kind and supportive, my aide—who had been Ahbi's aide before me—had an iron will equaling my grandmother's. I followed her with resignation to my dressing room, shoulders back, though the dance of upset in the pit of my stomach continued its waltz. I knew by the time I was dressed that dance would turn to a rapid tap and boogie, and hoped today, at least, I could avoid throwing up just before going to court.

Pagomaris was the only one who knew about my moments of weakness. And Ahbi, of course. My aide was trustworthy, at least, and kept my secret. Vomiting out my anxiety and frustration before each court appearance had become the norm, not the exception.

It hadn't started this way. In fact, when I'd been heir, things were far different than they were now. I held out my arms, allowed Pagomaris and her helpers to undress me as my mind remembered happier times. Being heir had been fabulous. After Ahbi's death and Dad's ascension to First Seat, I'd been left to observe my father and his Second Seat, my grandfather, Henemordonin, as they went about ruling Demonicon. I had the luxury then to disagree with Dad's choices, to scoff at his idea of "deomonocracy" and the reduction of power of the aristocracy. I thought I had lots of time to adjust, then. I believed Dad would be Ruler for centuries, at least. But only four years and I was thrust onto the throne when Dad abandoned us for his own needs.

I exhaled as Pagomaris firmly jerked on the lacings of

my black bodice and forced myself out of the self-pity that seemed to be my regular state of mind. I was happy then, when Dad decided to hand over the throne. I wanted to be Ruler, stood up to Henemordonin—no Grandfather title for him, either—and thought I could handle it. That I, at fourteen, could be Ruler of Demonicon and undo the damage my well-meaning but desperately wrong father had done.

Your father, Ahbi hissed and not for the first time, *is an idiot.*

Ahbi wasn't far off my own feelings about Dad. A further four years of impossible all my own proved me wrong. Syd's assertions I could handle it were so off base. Hayle or not, raised for rule or not, I should have paid closer attention to Dad's laws, to Henemordonin's eagerness to accept my father's release of control, to the court's equal willingness to seize as much power from the First Seat as they could. By the time I realized my mistake, it was far too late.

If you'd just listen to me, my grandmother snarled, *we wouldn't be in this position.*

Because challenging every single demon in court would make everything better. I held my temper with carefully balanced practice.

That's how things are done, she sent.

No, Ahbi, I sent, sighing. *They aren't. Not anymore.*

I was growing very tired of her constant whining for

the old days.

Pagomaris turned me around, clasping her hands under her chin, the shining black horns curving into her bright red tinted hair gleaming as she smiled at me.

"Stunning, Ruler," she said, bowing again.

I glanced in the mirror at my own horns, just beginning to coil with age, my glowing amber eyes, how my thick, black fingernails cut into the heavy skirt she'd draped around my hips. Gold and gemstones hung from everywhere, their weight pulling at me as surely as the pressure of my position, though I often took comfort from the snugness of the corsets I favored. At least they kept my backbone straight, my shoulders up. It was easier to face my doom with that bit of support.

It may have been the visit home, Syd's pep talk, or perhaps I simply was growing used to the tight ball of burning tension inside me at last, but I didn't throw up today. As I strode with confidence I didn't feel to the elevator that would take me to the throne room, my chin rose, my face falling into a blank mask of nothing and I thanked the elements for one day of reprieve. The birthday cake would have tasted worse coming up, I was certain.

You're a Hayle, Syd's voice whispered in my head.

You are Ruler, Ahbi chanted over my sister's memory as the platform ascended, Pagomaris behind me, two guards flanking my lead. Her pep talks always felt like orders. *Take control. You are Ruler.*

Made for power, Syd said. *I believe in you.*

Tears tingled as my sister's words drowned out my grandmother's voice. Syd believed in me, even when I didn't believe in myself. If only she knew the truth.

I braced myself for another round of humiliation and frustration as the platform came to a halt and deposited me at the top of the Seat. The porter bowed to me before turning to the gathered court, his power flaring.

"Her Royal Majesty," his words echoed back from the polished black stone and the invisible barrier leaving the sky open to the massive room, "Ruler of all Demonicon, Senne Hathenemeira."

I began my approach as the last word left his mouth, eyes forward, ignoring the stares of the gathered family, the whispers. I, instead, kept my gaze locked on my grandfather where he already sat in his throne, Second Seat just below mine.

What is he doing? Ahbi hissed in my head.

The need to vomit returned and, for a terrifying moment, I felt certain the birthday cake was coming up regardless of what I wanted.

Now, more than ever, you need to take control. Ahbi's harsh words slapped against my mind, suppressing my need to throw up just in time. Burning bile choked me, though my feet continued their long, steady stride, my hands unclenched at my side, expression unchanged. There were times I resented Ahbi completely, wished she would leave me. And then, there were times like this one I knew I would never survive this role without her.

What should I do? I wanted to hit him hard with all the power I could muster, the full pressure of Demonicon's magic square in his frowning face. How surprised he would be to suddenly find himself on the ground, pinned down by the energy at my disposal. How satisfying such an act, crushing him into dust beneath my feet. An image surged in my head, of doing just that. Of stripping him of his power, turning then on the gathered family and seizing control of my throne once more.

Do it, Ahbi sent. *Do it!*

It would be delicious and so satisfying. But fear quavered inside me, held me back as the consequences unfolded past the original idea.

What if I fail? I refused to meet my grandfather's eyes, to acknowledge him in any way as I approached, as though his lack of respect by remaining in his throne instead of rising to greet me meant nothing. I swept past him, spun and sat on First Seat and smoothly crossed my legs, hands settling on the familiar, cold stone of the throne while Ahbi raged at me.

At least you would have tried, she sent. And turned her back on me.

There has to be another way, I sent to her. *And we'll find it. We've spent four years being weak and losing control at every turn,* she sent. *Until you grow up and accept the fact nothing will change unless you act, we've lost. Just let him take First Seat and go back to playing at being someone important.*

Grandfather's power pressed down on me, his displeasure and judgment heavier than my own anxiety. I instantly blocked him, though the constant need to protect myself from him wore at me, the insistent chipping away at my resolve and nerve driving bile to the back of my throat once again.

What are you afraid of? Ahbi's scorn just made things worse.

Because I was afraid. *Dad left things in such a mess and I was so—*

"Now that Ruler has deigned to join us," Henemordonin said, voice heavy with disapproval, "court can commence."

My entire being clenched and hate engulfed me in arms of fury. I would never have considered myself a dark person, or one who acted on such emotional impulse. But the last four years had taken a toll on me and, as often happened when he pushed me too hard these days, the cracks let anger through despite my need to keep my head.

The power of Demonicon crackled out, slamming into him and washing over the court. Their collective gasp and stares tied to Henemordonin's eye-twitch didn't deliver the satisfaction I wished I'd felt from such a retaliation.

Instead, I just felt like a bully.

Now who's the idiot? Ahbi's mind shattered into rage. *Not that way, you young fool.*

And that was the core of it, the reason I was afraid. No matter what I did, I only made things worse.

Shock turned to muttering as my grandfather's mind tried to crush mine.

WE WILL SPEAK OF YOUR IMPERTINECE LATER. IN PRIVATE. He turned away from me then and waved to the gathered family as though he were Ruler.

And, choking on my mixed desire to kill him then and there hamstrung by my crippling fear of making things worse, I let him.

Chapter Three

"And so, you understand my position," the whiny, pathetic pile of uselessness standing before me said in his nasal voice, while his rounded paunch quivered in time with his words. "I can no more give up my present apartments to Pyeristericor," he glanced sideways at the thin, tall and scowling demon who shared the audience space at the foot of the throne dais, "than I could cut off my own arm."

"Perhaps I could help you in such an endeavor," Pyeristericor said, lips sneering at me as much as at the demon beside him.

Round belly spun with outrage on his red face, cheeks purpling in his anger. "How dare you!"

My lungs ached to sigh, my entire being craving the outlet of frustration and irritation, but I'd managed to endure the last several hours without showing any further signs of weakness and intended to keep it that way.

"Tilomyrins," I said to the still-quivering demon. "You claim you took possession of the apartments several months ago." If it were up to me I would never consider such trivial complaints. But Dad's insistence on demonocracy had led me here, to this moment, deciding which of these sad and sorry demons would keep possession of a stupid set of quarters no one cared about, including them. Considering they were both Fourth Plane and had quarters here on the Seat, a random set of apartments in the city could only be a petty attempt to wrestle some kind of concessions from each other. This wasn't the kind of garbage I believed Ruler's role was intended for. So why did I tolerate it?

One sideways glace at my grandfather's grim and serious expression sealed my fate for the remainder of this session. As long as he treated these trivial proceedings as though they required our full attention, I had to do so as well. Thanks to Henemordonin and his constant prodding, I was already on shaky ground with the family when it came to trust and respect. It didn't help matters one bit I now knew exactly how Syd must have felt when we were younger and she was struggling with her position as coven heir.

Thinking of her typically put me in a sour mood these days, but not today. Instead, when I thought of Syd, I almost smiled as I asked myself what she would do in this situation. For the first time since I took Ruler's seat, I allowed my sister's influence to rise and shine inside me.

You're a Hayle, her voice repeated and I realized only then it had been doing so in the background the entire time, drowned out by my fear and frustration. *I believe in you*.

Impulse, as powerful as Syd herself, seized control. Without thinking, channeling her on some deep level, I felt myself open my mouth and heard myself speak while Syd's voice rang in my head.

"Since you both claim ownership of the property," I said, "but neither can come to terms with who is, in fact, in legal possession, there is only one determination I can come to in this case." I almost giggled as mild hysteria at what I was about to do formed a spinning vortex in the back of my throat, a happy replacement to my need to throw up. The complainants both stared up at me with curiosity, though fearless. The demon in me wished I could lash out, knew Syd would have in a heartbeat. But I wasn't Syd, and had a position to protect and uphold. That didn't stop me from going on, however. "Without proper proof of ownership by either of you, I claim possession of the contended property and commit it to the holdings of the First Plane until such a time one of you can present me with evidence of your own claim."

Gasping raced its familiar trail around the room, whispering following the intakes of breath.

the planeless

Henemordonin looked up at me from his throne—a fact I knew irked him immensely—eyebrows pulled together. My nerves jumped, stomach clenching as the vortex of excitement collapsed. Had I done the right thing? He was going to yell at me again, I knew it. And though a little yelling wasn't such a bad thing from time to time, the fact I endured his abuse every single day wore on me so badly I could hardly stand to think of the little meeting he had planned for us after court was over.

All of a sudden such petty matters didn't seem so small or insignificant. I would tolerate hours more if it meant he wouldn't yell at me for a while.

But as my worries about my choice of decision bubbled and curdled, I caught a few nods, some smiles behind hands and felt the general approval of the gathered family of nobility. Even the two demons in question simply grumbled a moment, before allowing themselves to be guided away.

Consult with me next time, Henemordonin sent.

Like hell she will, Ahbi shot back. *Nicely done, Ruler*. I know she shared her words with him, because his cheeks reddened. I wish it made me feel better, but it didn't. The expectation of his yelling grew into an almost fever pitch of anxiety so powerful the tips of my fingers numbed from my grip on the cold stone of my throne.

You just need to stand up to him, Ahbi sent.

I've tried that in the past, I sent back. Fear quivered

through my mental voice and I was unable to stop it. *We tried yelling back for a long time. Then ignoring him. We even tried having him locked out of my office, remember? Nothing works. He just tracks me down and yells at me even louder.* I shuddered, the physical reaction to expectation crippling. *I hate this, Ahbi.*

There's only one way to end it, she sent. *You have to challenge him. Or kill him. I vote for killing him.*

We'd talked about this before and though it was very tempting, I couldn't bring myself to just have him assassinated. *What if we fail? He'd know it was me. Who else could it be?*

Ahbi sighed in my head, her presence feeling as defeated as I did. *I divorced him for a reason,* she grumbled. *Part of me forgot why. But he's much worse than he's ever been, the overbearing* juapunta. I almost snorted at the swear, picturing my grandfather as a spiny slime creature with twenty eyes and a bright pink tongue, notoriously stupid enough to eat just about anything.

It actually helped to have this conversation with her. *Killing is out,* I sent as the next set of demons began to speak. I pretended to listen as I paid close attention to my grandmother. *And if I challenge him… there's no guarantee I'll win.*

You have all the power of Demonicon behind you, Ahbi sent.

But I don't have the support of the court. Their constant judging and watching was almost as bad as Henemordonin's bullying. *Under Dad's stupid new rules, if I challenge him and win, the court still has the right to reverse the victory.*

I should have kept a closer eye on your father when he was Ruler. Ahbi sighed in my head, a sigh I myself longed to heave. At least one of us was able to expel our frustration. *I suppose this is my fault.*

I almost choked, covering my shock with a cough, winning me a glare from my grandfather. For the first time in years I wasn't focused on him when he showed his displeasure, ignoring him as Ahbi snorted at my reaction.

I can admit it when I'm wrong, she sent.

Of course you can, I sent, doing my very best to keep amusement from my tone, but knowing I failed terribly. *Happens all the time.*

We shared a laugh. And this time, when it was over, I did sigh, a deep and satisfying feeling. Yes, it attracted my grandfather's attention again. But all the tension was gone, to the point I flashed him a smile in answer to his overbearing scowl.

Can you tell me, I sent to my grandmother, *why the two of us haven't been on the same side all this time?*

She fell silent. I waited with more patience than I felt, wondering if she would even answer. When she did, her mental voice sounded muted, soft, apologetic.

I don't know, she sent. *These last four years haven't been easy for either of us.* It was hard not to empathize with her and I found myself reaching out to embrace her with my power as she went on. *Going from Ruler to living in your sister's head the way I did, it's a wonder I'm still sane.* I had to agree with her there. When Ameline Benoit killed Ahbi and framed Syd for our grandmother's death, Ahbi's first act had been to geas Syd with finding and killing her murderer.

I can imagine, I sent, not a trace of sarcasm making it past my sympathy, though I know I had every reason to be sarcastic. I'd lived with Ahbi tied to me far longer than the few days Syd had to tolerate.

I know, Ahbi sent. *Being part of the Node was a life—and death—changing experience.* It was Ahbi's tie to the core keeping Demonicon together I remembered the most vividly. Coming out of my forced addiction to nectar, moving here to my home, being part of demon society had been made all the more wonderful thanks to Ahbi's presence in the Node. But, yes, I had to admit, she really was different then. When Ahbi left the Node to join Ameline in the fight to stop the evil sorcerers, the Brotherhood, I missed her terribly. But the demon who returned was darker, angrier and, when Dad abdicated and made me Ruler, the full weight of Ahbi's presence settled inside me as though I'd swallowed her whole.

It must be so hard for you, I sent, waving absently as Henemordonin stared. He finally turned back to the two complainants and did his Second Seat duty. A flicker of understanding pierced my conversation with Ahbi as I realized this could be a regular thing. He'd tried to saddle me with the responsibility of all these tiny complaints, and I'd allowed it. But now I saw just how foolish and untrained that response had been even as, in my mind, I saw Syd's wry smile.

Why today? Why was it her concern and her words stuck with me now when they never had before?

You are a Hayle.

Because I was finally willing to listen and accept my older, braver, stronger sister really wasn't judging me. I was the only one doing that. Well, me and Ahbi. And Henemordonin and the rest of the court, not to mention all of Demonicon...

You are a HAYLE. My mother's daughter. My sister's blood. I'd let my grandfather make me forget who I really was.

My fault again, Ahbi sent, interrupting my half-amused, half-disgusted epiphany, as though out of touch, for once, with where my thoughts were going. *But you're correct. Let him deal with the mess he's made worse. If he wants the power to rule, allow him to rule—but only those issues that don't carry weight.* She laughed out loud, ringing in my head. *Actually, darling girl, it's brilliant. The court will see you being generous in your actions, and yet anything important that comes up, you take control.* She continued to chuckle before falling silent. *I'm a damned old fool, Meira. We could have done this long ago.*

My eyes burned with more sizzling tears, partially

from the relief I felt having her speak to me this way, but mostly for the lost time we'd allowed to pass. Lost time I'd allowed to pass, not only between Ahbi and myself, but Syd and me. And time I could have lived as the Hayle witch I was raised to be. Yes, I was Ruler of Demonicon. But four years of abuse beat out of me the truth—I was a witch as much as a demon. *No*, I sent, the sinking feeling I was correct making me a little ill, but only out of guilt even as threads of hope burst to life. *We needed to come to a place like this one in order for such a plan to work.* I couldn't help but send a little, *thank you, Syd,* into the ether. *I am a Hayle. And I'm done being pushed around.*

If anyone asks, Ahbi sent, *this was our contrivance all along. A few years of lulling him into submission and then BAM! Take his ass down.*

So that's how you always came across as so clever, I sent.

She shifted inside me, good humor filling me with calm for the first time in a very long time. *Even Ruler has her secrets, pet*, she sent.

I knew then this was how being Ruler was supposed to feel. I'd craved this feeling of belonging and acceptance, of being equal to the task. Did my grandmother's approval really mean that much to me? I was lying to myself if I thought otherwise.

I haven't made it any easier for you, Ahbi sent as Henemordonin pronounced his decision though I didn't hear a word of his choice. *And no, having my approval shouldn't be a priority. You are Ruler, Meira. I need to remember that.* She sounded so sad and distressed I softened further.

Grandmother, I sent, using that label for the first time in years, *we're both responsible for this. I think...* it was so difficult to go on, but I had to speak, at least to her, the fear I'd carried since I took Ruler's throne at fourteen. *I think Henemordonin is right and I'm too young and too untried to rule Demonicon.* Syd was right about many things, but in this instance, I worried she was wrong. I might be a Hayle, but she was the one raised for power, not me.

Ahbi snorted, batting at my power with hers. *Age has nothing to do with it*, she sent. *You were raised by Miriam Hayle.* Her echo of what Syd said earlier made me perk. *You know what being in control looks like. And yes, there have been hiccups.* That was what she called this disaster of a reign? *But overall, you've done amazingly well, considering the road blocks you've faced at every turn.*

This was such an abrupt about face I could barely breathe. Excitement rose once more at the possibility things might be turning in my favor at last. My birthday visit to Syd's was a good thing after all, a chance for Ahbi and I both to shake loose from our preconceived notions of each other. All because of my sister and my willingness to let go of being so darned stubborn about letting Syd in.

Any opportunity I had to continue our conversation was shattered when Henemordonin turned to me with an expectant stare on his darkening face.

I believe he asked us a question, Ahbi said, still amused though my fear tried to make a fresh appearance. I felt her push to the forefront. *May I?*

We'd fought many times over her attempts to take control of me physically in the past and I'd always been left resentful and furious while she slunk to the corner of my mind and stewed. But this was the first time she'd ever come out and asked.

Hope bloomed we could work together after all as I accepted, with a measure of relief, allowing her to feel part of the reason I always fought her was out of fear I wasn't good enough.

She hugged me as she took over. I could still see out of my own eyes, but felt her right there with me, everything in hyper contrast as the two of us shared my vision. My lips parted, feeling dry as she spoke, but the deep and condescending tone she used was all Ahbi.

"Speak up," she said as the family tittered in response. "And stop mumbling."

Hysterical laughter formed a bouncing ball of nerves right under my ribcage, making it hard to draw a full breath as I waited for his response.

Henemordonin's amber eyes flared with fire, his wide jaw clenching under his silver beard. I waited for the attack I knew was coming, the yelling and the fury but, in a day of amazing firsts, I felt my anxiety lessen and fade as Ahbi faced him down.

As *we* faced him down.

I saw him retreat, the anger in his eyes pulling back. He must have known Ahbi and I had come to some agreement and I made a further connection as he spoke. He'd been manipulating our lack of cohesion, using it against us at every turn.

No longer, Ahbi sent.

No longer, I agreed.

United—at least for now, because I held no illusions about either my grandmother or myself—we both listened carefully as he opened his mouth.

CHAPTER FOUR

"As I've already said," fire crackled in his amber eyes, "there is one matter you've yet to address." Henemordonin's lips lifted at the corners, though his face held nothing of positive nature in it. "That of your single status, Ruler."

Again, I caught myself thinking of Syd and how she'd been bullied into marrying Liam. I know she loved the sweet Gatekeeper, despite the fact he wasn't her first choice. His death had almost broken her, regardless. Now I was in control of my emotions again, I was very happy for my sister was finally able to wed the perfect man for her.

He's like a spinning top, your grandfather, Abhi grumbled. *You're a girl, yet.*

I'm Ruler, I sent as I considered my answer. No longer

the terrifying grip of fear or the irrational sharpness of anger dominating my thoughts, but the calm and rational patterns I was accustomed to. Syd was known for her reactionary nature while I did my best to think things through. Yes, I may have wished I was more impulsive, more like my powerful and decisive sister. And yet, I couldn't bring myself to simply act on impulse. *I must choose someone sooner or later.*

Ahbi grumbled in my head while I held onto my best blank expression and hoped my grandmother wouldn't backslide into old habits when I needed her support the most.

"I am well aware of the fact I have yet to mate," I said. "Are you feeling well, Henemordonin? This need to repeat yourself stirs concern for your mental health."

Did I really just zing my grandfather? The spinning excitement mixed with hysteria returned and, in that moment, I understood the siren call of impulse. No wonder Syd loved it so much. The freedom of speaking without censor liberated me like nothing else.

My grandfather may have tolerated Ahbi's snark, but it was clear he knew the difference between us. Even as Ahbi chuckled inside me, Henemordonin slammed both fists down on the arms of his throne and glared.

"You mock our laws, Ruler?" I had no idea it was possible for that level of disapproval to fill one demon's voice, so thick and sticky I felt dirty. Guilt fed by nerves fought against my need to keep control of the situation even as my grandfather continued to speak. "You treat this matter as though it amuses you. But we, as a people, look to you as an example for all demon kind. Such irreverence is insulting—nay, heartbreaking."

Ahbi sighed dramatically while the court shifted under his words. I felt the soft pressure of his magic, knew he used it to manipulate them as he often did. I hated such manipulation was only against the law for me, since Dad's rewrite of demon legislation was not complete. And, for as long as Henemordonin sat on Second Seat, it never would be.

The gathered family knew they were being played, allowed it to happen, that much was obvious from their eager anticipation of what came next. Excitement died a painful death in my heart, exchanged with dread and anxiety so powerful I had to force the saliva filling my mouth past the giant lump now blocking my throat.

This was the point I usually caved, gave in and retreated. But I'd had a taste of what things could be like and, with a searing need to recover that feeling spurring me on, I reached out with my power and cut him off from the court.

They gasped as a group while he slammed back into his throne, eyes huge, jaw jumping under the silver of his beard.

"You dare!" He spluttered convincingly enough,

despite the fact I knew his outrage was an act. I saw the cold calculation in his gaze, his realization something major had changed. Seeing his sophistry in such clear and conniving terms, after being pushed to my limit so many times, the last of my fear of him cracked and crumbled as my anger rose to the surface and took over.

"Challenge me," I snarled. "Just try it, Henemordonin. I'll crush you like a bug."

Ahbi crowed in delight as the entire throne room fell to silence. I didn't care, my focus fixed on my grandfather, his flow of emotions clear in his eyes as I watched him go from shock, to fury, into a moment I was certain he would act. When he finally looked away, his amber gaze shone sullen.

I swept to my feet, giddy with this victory, keeping my face flat and blank only through sheer will.

"Court is adjourned." I ignored them all as I strode from the room, knowing the balance of power finally shifted in my favor.

You've just made him more dangerous, Ahbi sent, but she didn't sound angry or upset. In fact, she seemed downright eager.

Let him come, I sent back as the elevator carried me down a floor to my living quarters. I moved before the platform came to a halt, stalking my way toward my office door, refusing to allow anything or anyone to slow my forward momentum. I had a sick feeling when I finally did come to a halt, I'd fall apart and there was no way I was doing so out in the open.

The two guards outside the double doors saluted as I pushed the portals wide with my power, slamming them shut behind me the moment I was through. My lungs burned as I gasped a breath of air, throat tight once again, eyes on fire with the need to cry, held in only at the sight of the tall, handsome demon leaning with his arms crossed against my desk.

Seeing Rameranselot here, now, only made matters worse. I stumbled to a halt, palms pressed to my thighs, thick fingernails digging through the heavy vinyl of my skirt as I fought to keep my composure. Why did he have to appear so sympathetic, his perfect face frowning in empathy even as he pushed off from my desk and crossed the distance between us, glowing eyes full of worry for me?

My heart soared and crashed, beat after beat, longing for him with a passion so vibrant I thought it would one day leap from my chest and land at his feet, even as it blackened and crisped in anger toward him for not being the demon I needed him to be.

Ram slowed before reaching me, jaw clenching as he came to a halt only a foot away, face hovering over mine. The scent of cinnamon and hot, delicious desserts washed over me. I hated Syd so much in that instant, knowing she'd kissed his lips when she'd considered him as a possible mate, no matter how irrational the emotion. Ram was mine, and yet, he wasn't.

"Might I say," he spoke, deep voice soft and full of subtleties I couldn't unravel with him so close to me, "that was very well played, Ruler."

He was there? "Was it?" The words blurted from my lips before I could stop them, the quivering I tried to halt taking over as his sympathy finally won through the crust of protection I tried to keep between us.

Ram's hands lifted, one cupping my cheek, the burning of his touch loosening my traitor tears. "It was a long time coming. And he deserved it."

I pulled away as his thumb traced over the line of moisture on my cheek. Ahbi sighed when I spun away, crushing my need to sob on his broad chest, to let out my frustration and the remains of my tension on someone I knew would never judge me.

"It was foolish," I shot at him, feeling my fear rise again. My body quivered at the memory of Henemordonin and his yelling. What was I thinking, challenging him?

We'll be fine, Ahbi sent.

You're not the one who has to face him, I snapped back.

"You know how I feel about Second Seat," Ram said, voice still mild though with a hint of anger breaking through his normally jovial tone. "And his treatment of you, Ruler."

"You've made it very clear more than once." I sank into my chair, eyes locked on the stack of parchment piled in the center of my desk. "And, in doing so, you've also made it clear you don't think I'm doing my job."

Ram's sigh was echoed by a second one from Ahbi. She grumbled something about being childish in my head while the tall, handsome demon shook his head.

"You have no idea," he said.

I looked away, refusing to meet his eyes. Perhaps Ahbi's assessment was correct. I certainly felt as though I'd spiraled back into petulance. And yet, I couldn't seem to find my way out again.

Salvation from myself came in the bustling, furious form of Pagomaris. She burst through the office doors, hustling to my side with her face twisted in a mix of anger and sorrow. I straightened in my seat as she came to a halt beside me, kneeling next to me with her eyes snapping sparks.

"How dare he treat you that way, Ruler?" When I'd first met my aide, she'd been Ahbi's, a kindly and anxious-to-please demon whom I'd though nice, but rather weak. I had no idea she was so passionate in her defense of the one she served, not until the first time my grandfather challenged me. Of all the demons in my life, Pagomaris was the only shoulder I allowed myself to cry on. Her loyalty was without question and her protective nature made me feel a little better.

Not so today. I simply squeezed her hand as she pressed mine to her face.

"It's all right," I said, suddenly tired and just wanting to be alone for a little while. I could feel Ram's steady gaze pinning me in place and squirmed under it without meeting his eyes.

"It isn't." The door slid shut behind the tiny demon who joined us. Avenesequoia's hands wrung before her doll-like self, a delicately embroidered dress making her appear even smaller than she was. My dear Sassafras's sister seethed, more angry than I'd ever seen her. "Victory, my Ruler. At least, for now."

I bobbed a nod, did my best to pull together my emotions. Something about Sequoia's attitude always dragged me from my lingering depression. It was as though her word was more important to me than anyone's. Perhaps because of her lineage and the fact I missed her brother's furry face so very much.

"Thank you all," I said, standing, shaking out my hands cramped from the fisted state they'd clenched into without my knowledge. "It's a small step forward. One I wish I'd taken long before now."

"He's never given you a chance," Pagomaris said. "Your father—" She gasped, as if at her own boldness. "Forgive me, Ruler." She choked on her words. "I would never criticize him."

I pulled her to her feet, allowing my anger to come

out. "I'll do it for you, then," I said as I finally met Ram's eyes. "Ahbi and I have come to an agreement."

She remained silent while I crossed the room and stood looking out the window over Ostrogotho. The capital city of Demonicon stretched out below me, the view from the Seat never failing to stir feelings of pride in my heart. But today, today I found those feelings more powerful than ever and drew on the strength they offered.

"Your grandfather is a master manipulator," Ram said, coming to stand next to me while Sequoia joined me on my left. I felt Pagomaris hovering behind us as he went on. "A lesser Ruler would have crumbled by now, Meira. In fact, your father did. It amazes me how well you've held up under such constant pressure."

I gaped at him, heart pounding. "You're kidding me, right?" I considered myself an utter and total failure to this point.

Ram shook his head, the light of the falling suns catching his curving horns. "Why do you think Henemordonin fights you so hard? You've held far more ground in four years than your father was able to in a month." Ram's smile crinkled the skin around his eyes, showing off his white teeth. "You can't see it, you're so deep inside. But those of us who watch can see the frustration in him, how desperate he is to control you. And how frustrated he is he's failed for so long."

Now I really needed to cry. My body swayed as I

reached out and clutched his hand while Sequoia rubbed my back in soothing circles with her tiny hands. My mind spun as I tried to process what he'd just said, to believe him.

"Why have you never said so before?" His hand squeezed back as I leaned on him for more than just physical support, our magic mingling around the edges as I let go of my rigid control for a moment.

"I have, silly girl," he whispered as he leaned in and pressed his lips to my ear. "You just haven't heard me until now."

"Ruler," Sequoia's voice broke through the hold Ram's breath on my skin held over me. I turned to look at her as she smiled. "We've been waiting for you to come back to us." Excitement rang in her words. "And now, you finally have. Haven't you?"

You can do it, Ahbi sent.

"I'm an idiot," I said, reaching for relief, finding only resignation. I'd made it this far. And my first victory gave me hope. "But I'm Ruler."

CHAPTER FIVE

Sequoia left shortly after, leading Pagomaris away. I let them go, sinking once again into my chair, hands spread out before me on the desk top. I'd grown used to the appearance of my red-tinted skin, the thick, black fingernails now with me full time. For someone who grew up hiding who she was the majority of her life, it had been a relief to come to Demonicon and shed my human disguise. Now, looking down on my demon hands, I almost wished I could go back and pretend to be normal.

No, you don't, Ahbi sent with such conviction I swallowed a lump of guilt. *And we both know it.*

She was correct, as usual, I realized. The idea of crawling back to the coven made my stomach ache and the hairs on the backs of my arms stir with rejecting gooseflesh. Being forced to hide what I was from infancy, unable to live as the demon girl that was my natural state, put a strain on me I didn't realize I carried until I moved to Demonicon full time.

A strong hand settled on my shoulder. I turned to look up into Ram's eyes as he sat on the edge of my desk and watched me with his usual calm stare. The same stare that, despite its lack of judgment, made me feel uncomfortable and awkward nonetheless.

He knew how I felt about him. I'd already confessed my feelings long before now, back when I was young and naïve, eager to prove to him and myself I was better than Syd, more than my sister. Ram's gentle rejection then broke my heart as much as his kind watchfulness did now. Because despite that initial rebuff, I couldn't help but feel the connection between us, in moments like this one, when his power wound around me in gentle support, guarded but softened enough I knew how much he cared for me.

I had two usual reactions to such closeness. Depending on my mood and the day, I either threw myself at him—something I regretted every single time, hating the sad denial in his face—or snarked my bitterness toward his rejection of us until he left me alone.

Change had finally overtaken me. This time, I refused to fall into bad habits. Instead of my usual, I tightened my stomach against my urgent desire to hug and kiss him and settled myself into my Ruler persona.

"Anything to report?" I purposely kept my tone soft, my body relaxed but for the rigid hold I had over my abdomen. One of Ram's eyebrows shot up into the hanging lock of his bangs, his power tightening around me a fraction. Was this what he'd been waiting for? He seemed to approve, settling himself more casually as he answered.

"Perhaps," he said. "There are murmurs of rumor. I don't have anything concrete."

I couldn't help but watch his lips as he spoke, jerking my gaze from their fullness as he finished. Ram had been Ahbi's eyes and ears in Ostrogotho. At times in the rest of Demonicon, as a spy and a patriot. He'd saved Syd and me when we first came to Demonicon, watching over us though we knew it not. When Ahbi died, instead of joining Dad's service, he transferred to me, his loyalty unwavering. I always found his jump from Ruler to heir odd.

I stood, crossing my arms over my chest, irritated by the fact when seated I had to look up to meet his eyes. Instead, we were now level as I spoke, grateful for something to distract me.

"That's the best you can give me?" I held my ground, resisting the urge to close the gap, to press my mouth to his, so near. It would only take a forward sway, a simple movement to lock my lips on his flesh. I think he waited for me to do so, expecting it, from the guarded look in his eyes. But when I didn't act, when I continued to wait and observe, feeling my personal power growing by the moment, Ram smiled.

"You know I'll tell you everything when I have information to share," he said. "My Ruler." His voice dropped in depth, his power heating around the edges of our connection, sparks firing off in his amber eyes. I felt my pulse increase even as I continued to hold back while I wondered if I was correct, that this was what Ram had been waiting for all along.

The thought made me angry and impulsive. Before he could respond, I lashed out and punched him in the shoulder, hitting him so hard he rocked back away from me. When he steadied himself, his eyes went wide, mouth hanging open.

"You jerk." I wished I could claw at him or hit him again, but I knew if I did I'd end up hurting him as he deserved to be hurt. "You've been playing me."

Ram's mouth snapped shut, hands reaching for me as he stood. I didn't pull away as his strong grip settled on my upper arms, handsome face frowning down at me though without anger.

"Meira," he whispered over my mouth, calling me by name for the first time in four years, "forgive me."

My nostrils flared as my power pushed back against his. "Forget it," I snapped. "Forget all of it. I see through you, now. I wasn't good enough—"

His mouth devoured my lips, arms pulling me against his chest as hunger rose between us. I dug my nails into his back through the thin fabric of his shirt, one leg hooking around his hip as I pushed him back onto the desk. Ram hit the surface hard, pulling me tightly toward him as his teeth caught my tongue.

I pulled away, panting, anger rising all over again. "Don't ever," I snarled, wiping my mouth with the back of my hand.

He drew a shaking breath. "Meira," he said, reaching for me, his own guilt clearly visible. I watched his passion fade and die, replaced by resigned grief. "I swore to her I'd take care of you," he whispered. "I can't do that if my mind is clouded. But it's become harder and harder to resist you."

She?

There was only one "she" who fit the bill.

This time when I lashed out at him, I meant it, my nails drawing across his cheek. Ram rocked back, shaking his head as he straightened, a thin line of blood growing from the cut below his left eye. But he didn't look angry, only more guilty and his expression fed my own anger.

"Syd isn't here," I said, reaching for cold fury and finding it waiting. "And this is none of her damned business." I shivered with the reaction as passion clashed with fury. "I don't need you to take care of me, Ram. I need someone to stand beside me." To stand with me against Henemordonin, to take my grandfather's place on Second Seat. I needed a mate, Henemordonin was right about that much. But not just any demon would do. "I need someone I can trust." My anger drained into soft desperation as I sagged, hands falling to my sides. "I need you."

How I'd longed to say those words to him. He'd never allowed me to get this far, always cutting me off or deflecting when I came close. This time, Ram sat silently, a trickle of blood tracking down his face. He held still for a very long time as my body shivered and I struggled to take control. At least Ahbi was staying out of things. I could be grateful for that much.

Ram stood suddenly and embraced me again, pressing me tightly to his chest. I felt his body trembling, heard his thudding heartbeat in my ear as I hugged him back. But this time it wasn't for my own comfort. I felt it was a shared support, as though he needed me as much as I needed him.

"You know I can't be who you want me to be." His words emerged thick and full of pain. "I'm too low ranked to be your mate, Meira."

"Says who?" I looked up in to his eyes, though I refused to let him go. It felt so right, infinitely comforting to remain there with his arms around me, mine looped about his waist, though the sight of his blood—blood I'd drawn in anger—still on his cheek made me wince from guilt. "I'm Ruler. And there are no laws against it."

He looked as though he wanted to argue, but remained silent, for once.

It may have been my small victory earlier made me bold, but I wasn't about to allow this chance to slip through my fingers.

"You've been telling me to stand up for what I want," I said. "I've struggled to do just that, Ram. But I'm here, now, and I want you."

His lips lingered on mine again, this time gentle and sweet. I held back, though my magic twisted around his, longing to pull him close and never let him go. When Ram lifted his face from mine, I could see his denial, though I knew it long before then as his body tensed and his magic gently rejected mine.

I backed away, sagging, defeated while Ram finally lifted one hand and swiped at the blood on his cheek.

"My Ruler," he said, bowing to me. "Please believe I only want what's best for you. And any mating with me will bring you complications you do not need."

"What the hell does that mean?" I stomped one foot, knowing it showed my childish side, but unable to stop myself from expressing my irritation. "You tell me to be strong, to fight against Henemordonin, and yet all you give me are riddles and half-truths." I shook my head, turned from him. "It's time for you to go." Time now, before I did something I would regret, before I fell back into the old patterns. I would not give in to the past and my weakness, not when I'd gained this small ground.

"Perhaps you should speak to your sister," Ram said, the exact wrong thing to come out of his mouth in that moment. "She knows your dilemma."

I didn't turn around. My power slammed into him, the sound of his deep grunt enough evidence I'd hit the mark.

"When I want your advice, Rameranselot," I said, "I'll ask for it."

Silence hung between us. I longed to spin around, to apologize, but my newfound backbone refused to bend or relent. I held my place, the mantle of Ruler wrapped around me as I heard him shift, sigh and leave.

Chapter Six

My fingers ached from signing paperwork, shuffling through the stacks of soft parchment, sorting and filing the pages afterwards as Pagomaris hovered at my elbow. It shocked me at first, this mountain of mundane. Who would ever have thought demons resorted to hard copies of anything, considering the amount of magic we had at our disposal? And yet, as my aide informed me, there was a distinct need for solid proof—sealed individually with my energy—the laws and decisions of the court were available to be viewed by any who might challenge them.

There was a time in the beginning facing this giant stack of minutia would have made me squirm and grumble. But I'd grown to enjoy the quiet hours I spent, the scent of the freshly pressed paper, the thick ink, the sigh of each page and the scratching of the metal quill pen I used to sign my name.

the planeless

Senne Hathenemeria. Over and over, like a meditation, the scrolling utensil itself infused with the power of Ruler. Fulfilling this task helped still my churning thoughts, calming and relaxing me to the point, when the doors to my office swung open and Henemordonin stepped through, I was in a perfect state of mind.

I glanced up at him, the pit of my stomach the only part of me registering the fact seeing his angry face stirred old anxiety. Pagomaris stiffened next to me as my eyes drifted from my grandfather's disapproving frown—he wore no other expression I knew of—and to the tall, broad-shouldered demon following behind and to his right. Jabuticabron nodded once to me, my beloved Sassafras's older brother taking a firm stance behind Henemordonin as the Second Seat came to a thundering halt in front of my desk.

Sass may have harbored ill will toward his brother when they were younger, but Jabuticabron mellowed from what I was able to garner, advancing rapidly in the ranks of the Seat Guard. When I became Ruler, my first assignment had been to elevate him to the leader of my personal retinue and he'd never given me reason to doubt my decision. On the contrary, with Jabut watching over me, Sequoia slipping in to watch from the shadows near the arching fireplace, I felt as close to the protective and watchful gaze of my dear Sassafras as I ever did.

With their firm presence to bolster my already altered mood, I found, for the first time in a very long time, I was able to hold on to my temper and my fear and simply observe my grandfather.

Yes, Ahbi hissed in my mind. *See him as he truly is. Not a frightening* gherlich, *all tentacles and darkness, but just a demon. A demon beneath you.*

How odd it felt, this detachment as I sank deeper into the quiet I'd managed to find. Where once his reddening face made me nervous, now he simply appeared silly, a boy in an old demon's body, about to throw a temper tantrum. I almost laughed. I held back my amusement by a hair's breadth. The moment of crystal liberation engulfed me and I embraced it in return.

This. Yes, this.

Giddy with self-discovery, I settled back in my seat and allowed the corners of my mouth to rise as Henemordonin leaned forward, fists on the edge of my desk. His power pushed against me as it always did, only this time I felt not intimidated, but amused. So pathetic, his attempt to bully me.

Ahbi laughed. *Oh dear*, she sent. *I fear you're a monster in the making.*

The term made me shudder. I'd heard it as a young girl, the night Syd declared to our parents she refused to use her magic, refused to be a monster. I had no idea her statement stuck with me so powerfully, despite her later attempt to smooth the edges of her dislike. It was enough to blunt my humor, though I knew now nothing would ever push me back into the corner I'd resided in for the last four years.

My grandfather's deep voice crackled with power as he spoke. "What exactly do you think you're going to accomplish with such acts of public aggression?" Could he sense he'd lost control of me at last? Did he feel my contempt, my lack of interest in anything he had to say? I could only believe so as frustration and a shock of his own fear passed through his eyes.

He's afraid of me? The idea surprised me.

Of course he is, silly girl, Ahbi sent. *You represent the future and he is the long past. Only your lack of conviction has given him any kind of power.* She chuckled, evil and eager. *Time to finally cut the rug out from beneath him.*

I didn't bother to remind her she was as old school as he. And Henemordonin *was* still my Second Seat, at least until I found another to take his place. But, I was done being pushed around and treated like a child.

"I informed you long ago," I said, voice low and steady, "I wasn't going to allow you to control me." Forget the last four years, they never happened. "I've given you a great deal of leeway while I've learned what I needed to rule Demonicon well and completely. But your petulance and bullying, while amusing at times, will no longer be tolerated."

Ahbi's laughter made it difficult to concentrate.

Henemordonin loomed closer, power now forcing itself into mine so hard I had to shove him back to keep him from crushing me. My chair made a scraping sound on the stone floor as I surged to my feet and battered him back, a snarl on my lips before I could stop it.

He straightened suddenly, drawing his robe around him, clearly offended.

"Your unhealthy temper gets the best of you yet again," he snapped, though all the pressure of his power had vanished. Winning this battle simply fed my confidence even as he went on. "I always believed your father's choice was the wrong one." I hissed in a breath as Jabut took a sharp step forward, Pagomaris snarling a guttural warning. "I worked very hard to guide and shape you, to make you a strong Ruler." Never mind he spent the last four years undermining me while encouraging the demononcracy laws removing my power a slice at a time. "Now I see my original supposition was correct. You are far too weak to ever be a good Ruler."

Energy surged out of me, Ahbi taking form, her furious face cascading sparks over my desk as she thrust a wall of anger against Henemordonin.

Guiding her is my job, she sent in a crush of power. *I'm the only reason she hasn't become a mere figurehead to your ridiculous attempt to take over First Seat.*

"Evil one!" Henemordonin's voice thundered from

his expanding chest. "Your influence has led us to this madness!"

Their magic clashed, parted. Only my hasty shielding prevented them from setting my still substantial pile of paperwork on fire. I clamped down on both of them, realizing only then, with my grandmother's attention elsewhere, Henemordonin was right. Ahbi was as much a part of the problem as he was. I felt suddenly clear-headed and myself for the first time in a very long time. And, with that clarity, came anger, shame and the old determined optimism I'd clung to as the second, odd child of a coven leader.

"Enough." They spun on me as I contained them both, trapping their power inside mine. The magic of Demonicon answered eagerly, buffeting them with enough energy to make Henemordonin sway. I focused first on my grandfather. "The next time you challenge me, publicly or privately, I'm replacing you as Second Seat." My fist impacted the top of my desk for emphasis. He spluttered, but I didn't allow him to interrupt. "I am so sick of you, I'm ready to crush you like a bug. Please, just give me a reason."

"How dare you!" He wrestled with my power, his own battering at the inside of my shielding without result. "I'll have you removed for such insolence!"

Jabut's heavy boots rang on stone as he stomped to my desk, fury on his face. "Ruler," he growled. "One word and I will have him arrested."

I think it was only then Henemordonin realized how far he'd gone. I watched his outrage turn to worry and finally sullen withdrawal. He bowed his head, sparks still lighting his eyes though his power retreated from mine and he took on a physical stance of supplication.

"Forgive me," his words ground out between the tight clench of his jumping jaw. How much it must have hurt him to say those words. "I am simply over passionate in my need to protect Demonicon."

Jabut's eyes never left me, begging me to tell him what he wanted to hear. And though it was the epitome of tempting, I knew having my grandfather arrested would get me nowhere. He had enough support in court, he would weasel his way free in no time, leaving me to face the twisting lies he would concoct to make me look like the one in the wrong.

"You may leave," I said, sitting down and refocusing on my paperwork. I glanced up after a moment, feeling the heat of his glare, one eyebrow rising as I gave him my most cold stare. "Perhaps you need your hearing tested. Jabuticabron, if you would escort Second Seat from my presence."

My guard captain saluted and spun abruptly toward my grandfather. He didn't speak, but he didn't have to. While Henemordonin was a large and barrel-chested demon, Jabut had at least half a head on him, full plate armor making him appear even larger. Not to mention the magic crackling around him while he glared at my grandfather.

Henemordonin offered a stiff bow and swept from the room, Jabuticabron on his heels. I held still until my guard slammed the double doors behind the retreating demon before I sagged back into my chair and fixed my grinning grandmother's spirit with angry eyes.

"You're next." I stood again, circling the table, coming to a halt beside the sparking, fiery outline of her spirit. Her expression wavered as her humor faded, though her eyes held mine. "I'm done being pushed around, Ahbi." She opened her flaming mouth, but I cut her off with a slash of one hand, my power circling her. It had once been hers, the magic of Demonicon, and though it felt confused about our relationship, it answered to me instantly. "This was your idea," I said, tone softening as her form did. "Clearly your methods haven't served either of us thus far." I drew a long, deep breath and released it in a slow exhale, just so happy to feel myself again. "You're welcome to stay with me," I said. "But please, Grandmother. If I'm going to fix the mess we've made in the last four years, I need to be me."

She grunted before nodding. "I was just trying to help," she said.

"I know." I reached for her, ran my fingers over the edge of her spirit. "But I think we both see now how things have to be."

"You don't need me." She floated back, mournful expression hardening into despair. "But I have nowhere to go."

"Yes, you do." I opened my arms to her. "And I need you now, more than ever. But not to control me. To work *with* me."

She hesitated. "I can't help myself," she said.

I laughed and nodded. "I know," I said. "I see now I allowed this to happen. So, if you're willing to give it another try, just be prepared. I'm not going to be a pushover any longer."

As Ahbi watched me, I embraced my responsibility in all this. I blamed Dad for this mess, Henemordonin for being a bully, my grandmother for interfering and pushing me around. But I was just as guilty. I had a brain, a back bone, didn't I? I allowed my fear of making mistakes and not living up to my extraordinary family hold me back. A huge weight lifted from me, leaving me breathless and a little shaky as I smiled.

"Come home," I said. "We have work to do."

"And your grandfather?" Ahbi hovered closer. "What are we going to do about him?"

I felt her slip inside me, her spirit form disappearing as she fit herself carefully and respectfully inside me.

I don't know yet, I sent. *But I have no doubt together we'll figure it out.*

chapter seven

I shooed my posse from the room, closing the doors firmly on Pagomaris who looked at me with hurt longing as the double portals swung shut on her. My shoulders pressed against the carved wood as I closed my eyes and explored my newfound freedom.

Ahbi squirmed out of the way, suddenly careful of my space, enough I found myself smiling.

You don't have to hide, I sent, striding back toward my desk with a fresh sense of purpose.

She didn't comment, nor did I have the chance to broach the subject again, not when I felt the firm touch of magic against the veil just as it parted. I spun in place, catching my breath as I stared through the tear between worlds and into the dark basement at home.

No, not home. In Wilding Springs. My sister looked back at me, Syd's dark hair loose around her shoulders for once, free of her normal ponytail, blue eyes worried and full lips pinched despite the smile she tried to muster.

"Hey, Meems," she said. "Someone wanted to say goodnight."

It was only then I noticed the small faces peeking out behind her legs. Gabriel's hazel eyes blinked slowly, a sleepy smile on his sweet cheeks. Ethie yawed hugely, waving her little hand as amber flared in her eyes, her demon waking at the opening of the veil.

I didn't hesitate, slipping through the tear to crouch and hug my niece and nephew. Two sets of moist lips pressed to my cheeks, arms choking tight around my neck. Why did their simple, non-judging love bring tears to my eyes? I smiled up at Syd, seeing her clearly for the first time in years, not as someone I needed to match or better, but as the big sister who loved me no matter what.

Ethie giggled as I stood with them in my arms, towering over Syd in my platform boots, still in my demon form. Gabriel ran his fingertips over my left horn, the sparks of green Sidhe power waking between us making me shiver. I still possessed my witch magic no matter my disconnect to the coven, though I rarely tapped into it these days, my demon having dominance over my power. It was nice to feel the connection reopen. As I noisily kissed the dear boy, I realized that connection was a large part of what I'd been missing.

Ethie twisted her tiny fingers in the coils of feathers

bound in my hair, hanging over my shoulder, bow mouth bright pink in the low light. She reminded me of me when I was little and I could only imagine all we Hayle girls had the same look as children.

"Did you have a good birthday, Aunt Meems?" Ethie's power touched mine, a firm and confident pressure well beyond her years. Syd and I had never spoken of it, but there was much of our grandmother in Ethie and I suspected the magic Gram lost when she became a sorcerer, the same magic Syd carried for so long, somehow found its way inside the Hayle heir. Considering the fact I carried our demon grandmother with me, stranger things had been known to happen.

"I did," I said, my continuing smile one of the first real ones I could remember in years. My eyes met Syd's as Ethie laid her head on my shoulder. "Started out a little rocky, but it's rosy now, thanks."

My sister's head cocked to the side, but her anxious expression had faded and her own smile pulled at her lips. "Nice to hear it," she said.

I kissed Ethie before setting her down with a firm smooch for her older brother. Gabriel silently took his sister's hand and waved at me before leading the yawning girl toward the basement stairs. I watched them go, heart light, Ahbi humming happily after the retreating pair.

"Thanks for that," Syd said, hands digging into the back pockets of her jeans as her dark hair swung over her shoulder when she turned from watching them go. "They miss you so much."

"I'll have to make sure to see them more often," I said even as I reached out with one hand. Syd swallowed hard, lower lip trembling as she jerked one hand free and seized mine, pulling me toward her. I shifted in mid-move to my human form, hugging her as fiercely as she hugged me, sobbing once onto her shoulder before falling still again.

"I missed you, too," she whispered, voice choked up. "Meems." She pushed me back, breath hitching as she scowled. "I almost lost you once." I remembered. It had been so hard to live with my addiction to nectar, with the changes to my personality that addiction created and the guilt and self-loathing I felt falling victim to Sekaniphestat and her schemes. Sassafras's evil mother was long dead for her crimes, but the legacy of her experimenting on me lived on. A shiver of the old wretchedness reemerged, but I was too far past it to allow it to take hold again. "The last few years have been tough, I know." She let me go, chin falling as she shook her head. "I feel like I left you in the fire." She met my eyes, her own guilt as clear as the love in her eyes. "I think it might be a silly question at this point." Syd shifted from one foot to the other, brows coming together, though she was smiling again. "But I'm finally asking. Are you okay?"

A flare of my old jealousy woke, hissed at me to hold

back. Ahbi jumped on it as quickly as I did.

You're going to need support, my grandmother whispered in my head. *Not just mine. And she's the perfect one to lean on. You know it. I know it. Stubborn or not, Ruler or not, we both need to trust she's the last one who will make us feel small for asking.* I almost gasped at Ahbi's confession of need, turned it into a nod and slow inhale.

"There have been some... challenges." Giggles escaped me suddenly, ripples of humor fed by mild hysteria, the same hysteria I felt earlier. I rather liked it, the impulsiveness. Syd's lips twisted into a grin as I went on. "But today has been interesting." I exhaled all the air from my lungs, feeling young again. The burden of Ahbi's years and experience and the unnatural aging I'd endured after all this time carrying the weight of Henemordonin's disapproval and connivance vanished in the face of my sister's genuine worry. "I'm dealing with it."

Syd's hesitation made me want to hug her again. "Ruler," she said, tone and words so careful I wondered how much damage I'd done to our relationship being so self-absorbed, "I know you are more than capable—"

"I am," I said. "But I'm also realizing I've been trying to do too much on my own." Syd's relief shone on her face and made me laugh out loud. "You could maybe pretend not to be so relieved."

Syd laughed with me. "Yeah, sorry," she said. "It's just..."

I nodded. She didn't have to go on. "I was that obvious, huh?"

There was a time I loved my sister more than anything, idolized her, put her on a pedestal. And a time I despised her perceived perfection, her power and courage. But I think I preferred this feeling most of all, the feeling of being her equal without needing to prove it.

Syd shrugged, all casual. "Not a bit," she said. "Figured you had it covered."

We laughed again, together, before I sighed.

"I'm sorry," I said. "It's been rough. But, I worked some things out today. I think I'm okay."

"Funny how that happens." Syd reached out and hugged me again. "I'm here, any time."

"Me, too," I said and let her go, feeling her reach for the veil the same moment I did. I stepped back through the tear, waving as I transformed into my natural state, blowing my sister a kiss as the hole in the veil sealed behind me.

Somehow, seeing Syd, speaking to her, cemented my newfound need to step up. Young or not, faced with a mess or not, I was Ruler.

Time to start acting the part.

I spent the night tossing and turning, mind churning around ideas. Ahbi and I talked long into the dark of the moons, considering courses of action and discarding others.

First things first, she sent as I stared out into the night sky and the glittering bands of stars twinkling overhead. *We have to deal with your grandfather.*

And reverse the laws Dad introduced, I sent. *This demonocracy thing isn't working.*

Agreed, she sent. *But until we have Henemordonin taken care of, doing so will be nearly impossible. I hate to say it, but you need to choose a mate.* I sighed as she went on. *The first step in seizing power is placing your choice of partner on Second Seat. While Henemordonin will likely fight your decision to replace him with your mate, he will have no choice but to step down.*

Wait a minute, I sent, a chill running down my spine. I slipped from bed, sliding my robe around my shoulders as I began to pace. *He knows that's true.*

Of course he does, Ahbi sent. *It's tradition.*

Why then, I sent, *would he want me to mate? Wouldn't he, instead, choose to have me remain single so he can stay on Second Seat?*

Ahbi fell silent before running off a series of curses so vile I was breathless by the time she wound down.

I'm an old fool, she sent, voice bitter, crackling with anger. *He has a plan.*

I sank onto the padded window bench, hugging myself against the soft breeze I allowed through the shielding over the opening. "And I am a young fool," I said. "Perhaps this has been his goal all along."

To keep us unbalanced, fighting each other, she sent. *The mate ploy, pushing you off kilter, it's a ruse. He knows you will fight him on it and, in doing so, will "prove" to the court you are unfit to rule.* She fired off a few more curses. *It makes logical sense, granddaughter.* She paused before going on. *I'm so sorry, Meira.*

No, I sent, *please don't be. I think this might work to our advantage. He's spent the past four years manipulating us into a corner with certain expectations to the end result.*

Only your sudden awakening and my consequent smartening up has smashed his little strategy into a million pieces. She sounded smug, though slightly worried. *I want you to be careful*, she sent. *If his plan is close to fruition, it's possible he could become desperate enough to take action against you.*

Let him try, I sent, sinking against the wall, drawing in a deep breath of fresh air scented with wild flowers planted on the balcony outside my room. *We're ready for him, now.*

I finally went to bed after further discussion took us nowhere. But before I fell asleep, I knew it was time to find a way to go on the offensive and stop reacting to my grandfather's every move.

I woke refreshed and smiling, actually looking forward to the day. It was a strange feeling, uncommon and reawakened the near hysteria I'd felt the afternoon before. Even Pagomaris was smiling, her minions emanating happiness as they dressed me. My usual somber morning ritual had somehow turned into a boisterous and pleasant experience I embraced with my whole heart. No throwing up, either. I was more than happy to adjust to a settled stomach.

I heard the sound of talking from the dining room and, as I entered my private breakfast chamber, it was with a smile for my gathered friends and supporters. The power of Demonicon embraced them as I crossed to the head of the table and took my seat. Their surprise quickly turned to smiles. Sequoia squeezed my hand from her seat on my left while Ram watched me with glowing eyes on my right.

You were right to keep them close, Ahbi sent. *I didn't have this. I never allowed friends in my life. But I see now their presence brings you comfort.*

Jabut saluted before slipping into a seat next to his sister. It had taken a full year to convince him to join us for breakfast, and another six months before he'd learned to be comfortable eating in my presence. Even now, he moved stiffly, precisely, though I wondered how much of that was his training and how much his need to show me he held me in high regard.

"Ruler," Sequoia nodded slowly to me, releasing my hand. "I take it some changes are in order?"

It was clear they sensed the difference in me from the anticipation on their faces, their sudden tension. Pagomaris watched with a brilliant need that made me smile.

"You are correct," I said to their collective sigh. It was the first time I had ever seen Jabut smile, a beaming expression lighting his entire face and reminding me of Sassafras's human form.

"I'll have him arrested at once." The giant guard was almost to his feet before I waved him down.

"That won't be necessary," I said, grinning at his disappointment. The chair groaned beneath him as Jabut sank back into it. "But there are certain steps we must take from this point on, and decisions to be made." I paused, meeting their eyes one at a time before continuing. "I value all of you, more than you know and am so grateful you've stood by me no matter my early failings." Pagomaris and Jabut squeaked their denial, but I shook my head. "No matter," I said. "The point is, I know I have you to rely on going forward. And I won't be able to restore order without you."

Well said, Ahbi sent.

They all bowed their heads to me before the door opened and Pagomaris's minions entered, laden with breakfast.

I listened with a happy heart as my friends—my advisors, yes, but my friends first and foremost— chattered in optimistic voices around me, absorbing their high energy.

I finally turned to Ram as he leaned toward me, eyes

glowing. "You had something you were investigating," I said. "Mind not being so cryptic this morning?"

He nodded quickly. "As a matter of fact," he said, "I have further confirmation, though I need to leave Ostrogotho to explore the matter."

The gathering fell silent as we all listened.

"As odd as it might sound," Ram said, humor in his voice, "there are rumors of a religion forming in the outer planes."

I barked a laugh, my friends joining me while Ahbi snorted in my head. "You're kidding?" The very idea of demons believing in religion… the thought of sacrifice for the good of others, for trusting anything but power and science, was ridiculous. "How human." I didn't mean for it to sound insulting. I was half-human, after all. But the whole thing was wrong in so many ways.

Ram shrugged, winking at me before sitting back in his chair. "I only report what I know, great Ruler," he said. "And that's the word on the planes."

Centuries of demons being lured to my former plane, often to be slaughtered as devils and creatures of evil by one religion or another, cemented a hatred for anything to do with following a path of worship. Ridiculous. Besides, the only thing demons worshipped was power.

"Very well," I set down my fork and the long, slim blade better suited for gutting a carcass than serving as a breakfast knife before gesturing at him with grandiose arrogance. "I task you, Rameranselot, Lord of the Eighteenth Plane, with the quest of uncovering the truth of this religion."

He bowed in his seat. "As my Ruler commands," he said.

Breakfast ended with all of us in high spirits, though Ram lingered when the others departed for my office and our strategy meeting. The first of many, I had no doubt. I approached him almost cautiously, wincing at the cut still visible on his cheek.

"I'm sorry," I said, keeping my voice low. "About yesterday."

He shook his head, touching the mark with his fingertips. "I deserved it," he said. "You have enough to concern you without adding my foolishness to your responsibilities."

I wanted to argue with him. Instead, I shifted focus. "You'll be careful?"

Ram snorted, suddenly carefree again. It was the part I loved most about him, how casually confident he always seemed. "If there is anything to these rumors," he said, "I'll be very surprised. But you will be the first to know, my Ruler."

I watched him go while struggling to keep my light-hearted feeling, wishing he would turn around and come back to me, wondering what it would take to change his mind about us.

chapter eight

I joined my friends in my office and quickly filled them in on the revelations I had over the last twelve or so hours. Ahbi grumbled a little over it, but I refused to listen.

Your reticence is what's put me in a corner in the first place, I sent to her. *You just said yourself friendship is a foreign concept. Well, it isn't to me. And trying to do things your way has just made my life miserable. So, if you don't mind, I'm going to go back to what's worked for me in the past.* I hugged her power gently with mine. *It's not like I can make a much bigger mess than I already have.*

Jabut's look of absolute satisfaction at my plans to finally combat Henemordonin on my own terms filled me with more confidence than perhaps I'd earned, but it felt good to see my friends smiling and nodding. Though, when I brought up my concern about my grandfather's maneuverings around my mating, Sequoia was as perplexed as I.

"I have found this part of his strategy most curious," she said, tiny body pacing rapidly before my desk. "As you yourself said, Ruler, encouraging you to mate simply places him in a position to lose power, not gain it."

"Perhaps he grows tired of the responsibilities of Second Seat?" Pagomaris's weak smile faded as she shook her head, the tinkling of crystals dangling from her coiled hair counterpoint to her denial. "Forgive my foolishness," she said with some heat. "I know your grandfather better than that."

"Until we know what he plans," I said, standing from behind my desk, "I want all hands on deck, eyes and ears wide open. Any hint of his strategy will help us combat it when the time comes."

Henemordonin may simply be pushing you to choose a mate of his choosing, Ahbi sent. I shared this with the others, to which Sequoia frowned.

"But to what purpose, Ahbi?" My grandmother's adoration for the little demon surged. She was one of the few who addressed the former Ruler directly without thought. "We will find out what he has planned, never fear. For now, might I suggest you allow him to lead you further down the road than you have in the past?"

The shrewd tightening of her brows in her diminutive face made me grin. "If only I was half so sneaky," I said.

"You think he'll reveal his plan if I start to submit to his suggestions?"

"Not just submit," Jabut grinned at his sister, chuckling. "Make it your idea, Ruler."

Sequoia laughed, her amusement ringing through the large room. "Excellent, dear brother," she said. "How delicious. By taking his thunder, but doing as he wishes, you will undercut his authority on the matter and redirect power back to you."

Ahbi grunted. *Exactly*, she sent.

I didn't hear you suggest it. It was hard not to snap at her.

Probably because you refused to listen, she shot back before clearing her mental throat. *Sorry*.

Me, too. This was going to take some getting used to, our little alliance. And yet, I had much more optimism this morning than I had felt for what was the Age of Awful. Could it be I was entering a new phase of my rule? One where I was actually able to enact change and positive forward motion?

"I love it," I said, shaking out the heavy, jewel-crusted robes Pagomaris and her minions squeezed me into earlier. My hair coiled over one shoulder in a thick plait wound with the leathery hide of a *fulshur*. The giant, gentle beasts of the plains were known for their supple, yet iron-hard hides. If nothing else, I could use it to club my grandfather into submission.

"Jabuticabron," I focused on him as he pulled himself

to attention. "Do what you can to watch Henemordonin over the next few days. I've given him a bit of a shock, waking up like this. And Ahbi seems to think he may be desperate enough to try something physical if I'm not careful."

Jabut's face darkened to deep crimson as he saluted. "I'll die before he touches you, Ruler."

"I hope that will never be necessary." I turned to Pagomaris. "I've never asked this of you, my faithful aide, but I know you must have connections inside the Seat, among the servants and the unseen."

Why did I never think of that? Ahbi actually sounded shocked.

Probably because you don't see her as an asset. And neither did I. Until I remembered I wasn't alone. Things were going to work out very well, indeed, I had no doubt now.

Pagomaris almost hit the floor, bowing so deeply her hair crystals tinkled against the stone. "My honor, Ruler," she choked out the words. "I have long waited to serve you in this manner. You have only to ask."

"I knew I could count on you," I said. "Sequoia?" She bowed her head to me. "You have been a great comfort to me. But I would ask you to join my network."

"Spying is my favorite past time," she curtsied with dimples. "No one pays attention to the tiny demon. I will uncover Henemordonin's intentions, have no fear."

I didn't, not anymore. And I suddenly understood

how Syd was able to do what she did, how she could bring herself to face such impossible odds. Idolizing her and resenting her for her magic blinded me to the truth of her real power—the people she trusted to have her back.

I sent them out with thanks, Jabuticabron striding with new purpose out the doors, Pagomaris bowing her way after him, beaming. Only Sequoia hesitated before closing the portals and returning to my side. I stared down into her wide eyes, so innocent looking in her startlingly attractive face. Her parents had created her, the perfect little demon girl, a face she would wear her entire, long existence. But though the top of her head barely came to my shoulder without my platform boots, there was a core of strength humming inside Sassy's sister I had come to admire greatly.

"Meira," she said, voice soft, hands folded in front of her, "might I speak openly?"

I nodded instantly. She rarely used my real name, but when she did I knew it was important.

"You can put a solid end to Henemordonin's plans right now," she said. "By naming your mate."

My breath left my body. I knew exactly where she was carrying this conversation and I wasn't sure I was ready to have it with anyone. But Sequoia wasn't about to stop on my account.

"Rameranselot is an excellent choice," she said, voice level and steady, though she rushed through his name ever so slightly, telling me she was as nervous about this discussion as I was. "He would make a fine mate and an excellent Second Seat."

I was grateful for the long, flowing sleeves Pagomaris chose that morning, the cuffs hiding my clenched fists even as my heart swelled open. "He won't accept," I said.

Sequoia sighed, reaching out to squeeze my arm. "He will," she said. "For his own good."

Her insistent tone made me laugh. "I'm sure he'll see things that way," I said. "What a marvelous beginning to a marriage that could last millennia? 'Hey, honey, I know you don't want to marry me, but I'm Ruler, so you have to say yes.'"

Sequoia wrinkled her little nose, though her eyes sparkled. "How you do it is up to you," she said. "I would never interfere with such a delicate negotiation." I snorted as she went on. "You know I'm right."

She was, absolutely. And I wasn't exactly arguing with her. But I'd been raised on love and commitment and finding your soul mate, not marrying for position and power. Mom, Syd, even Gram's love renewed with the restored Demetrius Strong, set the stage for what I really wanted.

"I'll ask him again," I said, optimism fading. "Reason with him." The thought made my soul sigh in sadness. "And we'll see."

Guards stood at attention as I swept past them, down the long corridor to the elevator platform. I ignored them as Ahbi shifted and sighed inside me.

It's been a lot to adjust to in the last little while, I sent, my natural empathy rising for her. *But for the first time, I really think we'll be okay, Grandmother.*

I know you will, child, she sent, immediately making me wonder about the singular pronoun usage. But she went on before I could correct her. *It's not your awakening that has me anxious. At least, not directly. I've been so deeply invested in trying to control everything, I failed to realize just how different things are.*

I slowed my stride, feeling Sequoia match my pace without comment, eyes scanning the city outside as I stepped onto the platform and strode to the edge. The thick shielding protected me from a fall, though I barely thought of such a risk. I loved to look out over Ostrogotho, to breathe in the fresh air blowing toward the mountain peak, tempered by power to a breeze. *Dad's laws can be reversed,* I sent as the elevator bounced softly and began to rise. *Now that we're working together.*

Ahbi tsked. *No, Meira,* she sent. *I'm talking about the changes I made. And your sister. Don't you feel it?* She opened her power to me, and, in doing so, woke my link to the Node. A frown pinched my brow as she went on. *I suppose it's more apparent to me,* she sent, *considering how much time I spent as Ruler. And the fact you only took over after my stay.* Her death had done nothing to keep her down. She'd been right there with Syd, helped my sister save the Node. The power core holding all the planes together had been home to Ahbi's spirit for a while because of that battle to save Demonicon from destruction. She showed me the dull quiet of the old Node, how it seemed to have little personality and no interest in anything outside its own existence. I gasped as the elevator came to a halt, still turned away for privacy as I compared that feeling to the Node I knew.

Curiosity, a sense of purpose and a hint of emotion now colored the energy of the magic holding everything together.

Is this a bad thing? I knew the guards waited for me to leave the elevator, but no one had the nerve to interrupt me. Let them wait. Let them all wait.

I don't know, Ahbi sent. *I don't think so. But that could be my own ego. I'd hate to think I damaged the very thing I spent my entire life protecting.*

I felt the Node again, its soft enthusiasm and the budding life and liveliness as it swirled around me. The touch brought a smile to my face.

From what I can tell, I sent, turning at last, allowing my features to fall into blankness as I stepped past the guards and into the throne room, *you did good.*

We shall see, she sent, her pensive tone full of more worry than I thought her capable. *Of course I worry,* she snapped. *I'm not an empty soul, child.*

You do an excellent job hiding it, I sent, eyes front, locked on my throne. Who cared Henemordonin glared? Or that he repeated yesterday's performance, butt remaining in seat as I climbed the stairs without bothering to acknowledge him.

I suppose I do, at that, she sent. *Now, remember our plan.*

As if I could forget it, I sent back just as I spun and sank into my throne. The seat normally made my backside ache, rigid stone unyielding, making me feel unwelcome. But a touch of magic created a soft padding of power, a concession I'd never allowed myself before for fear of appearing weak.

Time to stop caring what they think, I sent to Ahbi, *and focus on my job.*

I felt Henemordonin's body gather momentum before he even moved, pinning him to his throne and silencing him with a burst of magic only the two of us were privy to even as I crossed one leg slowly over the other and settled back into another padding of power.

"Hear me," I said while my grandfather struggled against my control over him, "your Ruler speaks."

The gathered nobility of Demonicon, most of them related to me, bowed to me as one, eyes full of curiosity.

"I am young." I lowered my chin ever so slightly, a nod to their concerns even as Henemordonin tensed and fell still. "I have plenty of time to learn and grow as Ruler.

We demons are long-lived and, as my predecessor, Ahbi Sanghamitra, proved, the duration of Rule can extend over millennia."

Excellent, she sent. *Remind them of me and avoid your father. Let them remember what it was like to bow to their Ruler.*

I almost grinned. "I would prefer to focus on leading my people." My chin rose as I allowed my magic and the full power of Demonicon to flare around me, not so subtle, I knew, but necessary reinforcement. The court responded with a small ripple of fear, though their instant support, even if veiled behind lies and deceit, was far from mine. "While I have much learning yet to do, I have the finest teacher in all Demonicon to fulfill that training." Henemordonin actually softened slightly even as Ahbi laughed. "Ahbi lives yet inside me, her guidance and centuries of experience exactly what Demonicon needs moving forward."

The flat fury in my grandfather's eyes was imminently satisfying. So much so, it was tempting to rub it in.

Focus, Ahbi sent.

Of course. I went on. "Considering the fact I'm still training my Second Seat to carry out his duties to my satisfaction," a titter of laughter rippled through the gathered family, "choosing a mate and conducting his subsequent instruction is a daunting proposition."

Oh, very well done, my grandmother sent. *He may do us a favor and have a brain rupture.*

If only, I sent. "But, as it is the will of my people, and because I would serve you to the very best of my full power and capacity, I am prepared to select a mate." Another burst of magic reminded them who was supposed to be in control here. "A young and eager mind at my side, tempered by the will of Ruler, can serve as a catalyst to further change and lead Demonicon to even more greatness."

Dig the dagger in a little deeper, won't you, sweetness? Ahbi's humor was so dark I zinged her with some power to calm her down.

He's going to freak out at me, I sent as I observed the family nodding and smiling, chattering over my pronouncement with eagerness I hadn't seen in them before. *But it's worth it.* I saw him fuming out of the corner of my eye and released him from my control, fully expecting him to lose his mind.

Henemordonin didn't, to his credit. He was enough of a politician he must have recognized the way the wind was blowing when it came to the court. But considering this was his idea all along, I shouldn't have been so surprised he held his temper. At least, in public.

Look at them, Abhi growled. *How eager they are. You know they would be just as happy to depose you as they would to see you married off?*

Naturally, I sent, personally shocked at how calm I felt. *I don't know how you managed for so long, Grandmother. But*

I suppose I'm going to find out.

My dear, she sent, *you are, indeed.*

That encouragement meant more to me than she would ever know.

chapter nine

Though I'd accomplished a minor victory, it wasn't as long-lived as I would have liked. In fact, within moments of releasing control over Henemordonin, confrontation came, not from him as I expected, but from one of the gathered court.

When my cousin, Tanasharia, stepped forward, I had no time to stop her before she spoke up. My teeth ground together as I held my peace while her false charm oozed forward.

"Ruler," she said, silken voice barely hiding her contempt, "when can we expect to see you move ahead? Or is this a plan you have for some later date?" She glanced only for a moment at my grandfather, long enough for Ahbi to hiss in my head.

He needs a new mouthpiece, she sent.

She was the perfect choice to oppose me, and often

did. With the death of her brother, Cypherion, and her father, the former Second Seat, Vandelarious, at Syd and Dad's hands, Tanasharia had made it her mission to do everything she could to make my life miserable while remaining outside my ability to punish her for her actions. Subtle social bullying, outright confrontations disguised as family concern, and barbed jabs during court engagements were regular fare from her. I used to lump her abuse in with my grandfather's attacks, allowing her to pile pressure on me much as he did. But as I stared down at her, seeing through her thin attempt to be noticed, to stand up to me, I actually felt sorry for her.

"When you need to know," I said, dropping my tone to a deep rumble fed with power, the floor rippling under her feet in answer, "I will inform you." I allowed her to feel the pressure of my magic and watched as her normal smirk faded as I added weight until fear flashed in her eyes.

Enough playing, Ahbi sent. *She is not important.*

Oh, I disagree, I sent. *They are watching, are they not?* The entire court observed, silent and focused. *I've not only allowed Henemordonin to push me around, I've permitted it from one as lowly as Tanasharia.* Mind you, she was a Seventh Plane Lady, but she'd fallen far from Second Plane and I knew longed for her former place of glory and honor.

Tanasharia finally bowed to me, backing off. "Your will, Ruler," she said.

I flicked my fingers in her direction, a nuisance fly dislodged from my presence. I had no doubt she would continue to challenge me, but seeing how easily she was defeated, I knew I could handle her. Which gave me much more confidence Henemordonin was a tacklable problem as well.

"It is your Ruler's will," I said then, "all demon males of eligible age and rank come forth at this time to be presented as a possible suitor."

They weren't expecting immediacy from me, I could tell instantly. It took a full minute before anyone came forward, though once the first demon set foot in the center of the aisle, a rush of tall, broad-shouldered males joined him. Henemordonin shifted subtly in his throne. I knew it was probably best to resist poking the angry bull, but I couldn't resist.

So eager to be removed from power? I didn't meet his gaze, simply allowed the question to sit between us. *I'm happy to oblige you.*

Ahbi hissed at me, but Henemordonin's reply was as softly delivered as my query.

I only want what is best for Demonicon, he sent, stiff and formal. *The fact you've never understood that tells me your grandmother's influence has been detrimental to our cause.*

This time I did meet his gaze as he went on.

You see me as an enemy, he sent, with more softness than I knew he possessed, *and I wonder if Ahbi hadn't been between us, kept us from doing what we needed to, would things be different now?* Wistfulness didn't become him, in my opinion. *I suppose we'll never know.*

He looked away, leaving me with the sick feeling his words had been meant either as some kind of warning or just the opposite—a threat. I wasn't sure which troubled me the most.

My grandmother's silence spoke to her own concern, but instead of chastising me for prodding Henemordonin, she instead sent, *Ram isn't here.*

I hardly needed the reminder, I sent. *And this is a delay tactic, remember?* My gaze scanned across the cluster of faces, each increasing the churning regret in my stomach until I felt so nauseated I was certain I would lose all control of my digestion. *They can't be serious.*

Ahbi didn't need an explanation to understand my statement. *Most of these are cousins you would never consider,* she sent. *Either too close in bloodline or not powerful enough.*

And just disgusting. I allowed my lip to curl up, to express my disdain as I held onto my poise with all of my strength. *Most of them have, at one point or another, made it painfully obvious they either consider me too weak to serve as Ruler or too mis-bred. As if I would choose any of them.*

Only one stood out, literally and figuratively. Not only was he leaner than the rest, he didn't carry the typical massiveness of most demons. Instead, his body was more compact, his clothing tailored to subtlety instead of excess, no spikes or sparkling gems or even plate armor sewn into leather to accentuate his frame. I found his open, quiet gaze rather disconcerting, to be completely honest, and heard Ahbi's musing hum as I looked away from his handsome face.

I know him, she sent. *Elphremantic, I believe. Parents are Fifth Plane. Not the brightest demons, but he could suit the part if need be.*

How have I never met him before? I continued to sweep the gathered males with my gaze in silence, watching them shuffle in discomfort, though my face relaxed as much as my stomach as I dismissed them one by one.

Why don't we ask him? Ahbi prodded me gently and I found myself speaking, though with my own voice.

"Come forward." I gestured to him, maintaining my level calm. He did as I bid him, bowing deeply, but without the overly-fawning supplication I dreaded. "Your name and rank."

"Elphremantic, my Ruler," he said in a melodic voice, soft but firm. "Lord of the Eighth."

"You've been missing from court," I said. "What brings you back?"

"I had the honor to be enrolled in Teris Haralthazar's enrichment program, my Ruler," he said. "Ten of us were chosen to leave Ostrogotho and live among the lower Planes for several years, in an effort to teach us good leadership and understanding of the lesser classes."

I had no idea, I sent to Ahbi.

Neither did I. She grunted.

"I have just returned from Bilhaeder, my Ruler," Elphremantic said. "I'm honored to finally stand in your presence." I'd heard such declarations before, but his was the first that came across as genuine.

He's a possibility, Ahbi sent. *If Ram says no once and for all.*

We can at least present him as such, I sent. *Showing interest might create the illusion we need to uncover Henemordonin's plan.*

Very well, Ahbi sent, her approval clear in her mental voice and flare of magic. *A word of praise for him should be all the seed you need to plant at this time.*

I bowed my head ever so slightly to him. "Welcome home," I said. "I will be very interested to hear what you've learned in your time away from the Seat."

Their murmurs of interest were all I needed to tell me Ahbi was right. That simple statement gave the gathered court the rumor fodder necessary for me to now act with whatever speed I saw necessary.

Now, if only the way he looked at me didn't raise more of my interest than I'd intended in the first place, I might be able to actually get some work done.

Court went much more smoothly after my announcement. For whatever reason, the challenges and petty arguments either stopped bothering me as they usually did, or they really were fewer in number.

the planeless

It was a lovely surprise to discover only two short hours took care of the bulk of the issues and I wondered if this was what things were supposed to be like as Henemordonin stood.

Depends on the day, Ahbi sent. *But I do recall having more time to focus on study and investigation.*

You mean snooping and spying, I sent, though with a laugh in my mental voice.

She snorted as my Second Seat spoke, deep voice carrying with a hint of power.

"Our Ruler shall host a dinner this evening," he said while I swore inwardly at his presumption, not that I was really all that shocked to find he side-stepped my attempt to control things. He'd proved himself adept at such matters and I really had to be resigned to the fact I wouldn't be able to avoid his manipulations completely. "All eligible suitors are required to be in attendance."

He turned to me, flames rising in his eyes. "Ruler?"

I hate him, I sent to my grandmother as I stood and moved past him, already descending the stairs.

"Court is dismissed," I said, half-way down the center aisle on my way to the elevator before the chattering could start up again.

I don't know what you're so upset about, Ahbi sent as I sent the platform dropping toward the next level. *It's just dinner.*

I know. I stepped off, pausing to catch my breath as

the guards straightened into attention. *I think I'm so ready to be done with him, anything he does from now on will tweak my temper.*

Which he'll attempt to use to his advantage, Ahbi sent. There was a time, only a few short days ago, I would have taken her heavy tone as oppressive and controlling. Now, as I walked the long hall to my office, I, instead, chose to interpret it as an attempt at an education.

Thank you, she sent.

I was about to respond when I spun at the sound of footsteps following me. I expected Sequoia perhaps, or even Pagomaris. But the sight of Tanasharia's smirking face put me on instant guard even as I longed to use all the power of Demonicon to crush her out of existence.

You really are very much like your sister, Ahbi sent.

"Ruler." Tanasharia dipped into a curtsy, though barely deep enough to convey any amount of respect. Instead of saying anything, I stood there, staring at her with heavy-lidded eyes, waiting her out. Her fake smile faded as the seconds ticked past until, visibly flustered and not so sure of herself, my cousin went on in a rush of hasty words. "How delightful you've finally decided to choose a mate. Might I offer you some recommendations?"

What cold vault of frozen hell had she emerged from she thought I would ever, in a million years of rule, consider her a confidant?

the planeless

This must be your grandfather's influence, Ahbi sent, her amusement back again, heavily brushed through with contempt. *How pathetic of him.*

And how very little he really knows about me, I sent. *Maybe the past four years have served me after all. I think I've rattled him.*

Tanasharia shifted from one foot to the next, hands now clenched in the layers of gauze overlaying her skin-tight gold dress. I watched as her chest rose and fell more rapidly, eyes tightening around the edges as I continued my conversation with my grandmother and went on ignoring my cousin.

It might be wise to confide in her, Ahbi sent. *But even I wouldn't encourage you to such falsehood. Neither of us would be able to maintain the subterfuge for long.*

I had no idea how effective simply staring at someone could be. Tanasharia had worked herself up to licking her lips, shoulders shrugging as though in an effort to shake free from my glare.

You might want to cut her loose at this point, Ahbi sent. *Too much of a good thing?*

I hated to waste the chance to crush my cousin, but my grandmother was probably right. "I'll take your offer under advisement," I said, my tone leaving absolutely no question I would do so only under the harshest of duress.

Tanasharia cracked, snarling at me. "You think you're so powerful," she hissed. "We'll see how long that lasts."

It would have been simple to gesture to one of the

guards and have her arrested. I knew the new laws wouldn't allow me to have her stripped and killed any longer, but I could at least have put her into an uncomfortable position until someone finally rescued her from beneath the Seat.

Instead, I let her go as she spun and stomped off, turning my back on her and continuing to my office with a growing worry in my heart.

An empty threat, Ahbi sent, though even she felt hesitant.

Of course, I sent.

I pondered my cousin's words that afternoon in my office and into the evening as Pagomaris dressed me for dinner, alone when Ahbi retreated from my conscious mind as she sometimes did. Tanasharia was in Henemordonin's confidence, that much was clear to me, though how much he told her remained to be seen. If I were my grandfather—the elements preserve me from ever becoming like him—I wouldn't have told the nasty, impulsive demon girl very much. Knowing Henemordonin, he was smarter than that, but I could hope to wring some further benefit from her if the time came for a full-on confrontation with my Second Seat.

It shocked me when I realized what I contemplated. War between Henemordonin and myself. And yes, I really did think it could come to that, if I let our conflict go too far. I'd eased up on my own guilt, but my anger at Dad and his foolish attempt to change the way demons were ruled rose as strong as ever.

Sequoia entered after a few moments, bowing to me. "I thought some insight into your suitors might be welcome?"

I nodded, grateful for the distraction, though I couldn't help but wrinkle my nose at her as she sat on the edge of my window seat, feet swinging beneath her.

"If we must," I said. "Tell me this dinner won't be a complete disaster?"

Sequoia laughed, brightening my mood with the sound of her chiming voice. "No promises, Ruler," she said as her hand traced a path over the air beside her. While my work was all done on paper for posterity, most demons kept track of their day-to-day schedules with magic. Sequoia's smooth, flowing hand writing appeared in glowing amber lines as she perused her hovering notes.

"Let's see," she tapped a line of writing. It shifted and reformed, the image of a demon appearing next to her sparking words. "Most of the cousins are out, am I correct?"

I shuddered as two minions slipped a silky pair of fingerless gloves over my hands, but not from the feel of the fabric. "Please."

Sequoia bobbed a nod, her horns appearing through the pile of curls bound in two grape-like bunches over her temples. "That leaves six candidates," she said. "Two are,

I believe, unsuitable due to age." She flicked past their images, the demon's faces appearing and disappearing in her magical Rolodex. "And two are previously mated, though now single again." She met my eyes. "While there are no laws against it, I'm thinking perhaps an unwed suitor might be more desirable?"

There was nothing wrong with marrying someone who'd been mated before. But I did feel my bias leaning toward someone who had as yet to experience being partnered.

"And someone young, please," I said, turning as Pagomaris guided my body, her demons hard at work.

Sequoia sighed, hands dropping. I looked up to find two faces hovering in front of hers. One I knew very well, had kissed his lips and longed for more from him. Rameranselot might have been Eighteenth Plane, but he was in the running, I was happy to see.

The other sent a tingle of surprise and a thread of guilt down to my belly, if only because I hoped he'd be on the final list. Elphremantic's enigmatic smile flickered in amber flame as Sequoia waved both demons out of existence.

"Well," I said, "nice to know I have such a wide selection to choose from."

Sequoia's little smile hurt as much as Ram's silence. I hadn't intended to ask her, but the question slipped from my lips none the less. "Is there any word?" He'd only been gone since breakfast. I really was a silly ninny. But all of this agreeing to mate talk had him in the forefront of my mind all over again.

"Nothing yet," Sequoia said.

Which meant he would be missing this evening's festivities, leaving me to deal with a pack of demons I wanted nothing to do with. Scowling at my reflection as Pagomaris offered a full-length mirror, I vowed to myself to have an absolutely horrible time.

chapter ten

There's something to be said for self-fulfilling prophecies. Ten minutes into dinner and I was ready to move on from this disaster and pretend it never happened.

The small dining room on my apartment level had been lit with what I could only imagine Henemordonin considered romantic lighting—at least a hundred looming candelabras in the shapes of drach and other monstrous beings wearing wreathes of magic powered candles. A long row of miniature matching holders ran the length of the long glass table, the underneath vista a bubbling volcano. The visual was so realistic I could almost feel the heat rising from the surface. While the candlelight alone may have accomplished my grandfather's aim at setting the mood, when paired with the boiling, reddish tone of the lava, he merely succeeded in creating lighting masks of horror cast over every face, a macabre scene sending shivers down my spine.

"How unfortunate," Sequoia murmured at my side, hiding a smile behind her diminutive hand.

At least I wasn't the only one who noticed.

My grandfather already sat at the far end of the table, the glow from the glass making him look like possession was the least of his problems. I didn't bother to acknowledge him as the royal page announced me, instead striding immediately to my seat. Four of the gathered demon males attempted to pull out my chair for me, only to be firmly accosted by Jabut and his guards.

A sigh of frustration clenched tight in my chest as I did my best not to allow it to escape.

Sequoia sat next to me, on my left, though I had little choice as to who had the seat on my right. I was grateful to have my friend with me at all, her presence offering some small respite from the hungry stares of the gathered demons. I expected Tanasharia and her friends to crash my little party and she didn't disappoint. Sprinkled among my suitors sat a variety of stunningly beautiful and powerful young demon females, all flirting outrageously with those who were meant to be my picks for mate.

Tanasharia didn't meet my eyes, so I could only guess she yet struggled with our earlier meeting. Being in a crowd of her peers would make her bold again, I had no doubt. For once, I didn't care how she acted or reacted.

As far as I was concerned, this dinner was nothing but a farce to satisfy my grandfather and the court long enough for me to convince Ram to marry me.

"My Ruler," Elphremantic had somehow managed to claim the right hand seat, glares from his fellow demons telling me, with no uncertainty, he'd fought hard for the privilege. "Allow me." His slim hands personally poured me a sparkling glass of *vrena*, what amounted to wine on Demonicon. I ignored him though, as I sipped my drink, I remembered he was my only other viable alternative.

Isn't he delightful? There had long been a ban on mental communication on Demonicon, a way for Ruler to control attempts at coups and contrivances. The law was broken frequently. It had been broken, in fact, by Syd and I the first time we visited. Unlike my grandmother, I chose to encourage my people to speak with me through their magic. This situation was a case in point in absolute favor. I didn't have to glance at Sequoia to know she spoke of one of the demon males who aggressively stuffed dripping meat into his mouth so quickly he barely chewed.

Delicious, I sent, setting aside my own fork, appetite lost at such a sight.

And dear Tanasharia, Sequoia's mild tone layered deeply with sarcasm and wit, *always a class act.*

My cousin encouraged the demon next to her to eat a bite of bread from her very large chest while laughing so loudly my ears ached.

I'm surrounded by the epitome of polish, I sent.

Ahbi snorted in my head. *Just look at him*, she added her own commentary. *Sitting at the foot of the table like he's Ruler himself, ignoring the mess he's making.*

She was right about that. Henemordonin ignored the growing noise, the increasing antics of the young demons, quietly devouring his own meal as though nothing was amiss.

What is he up to? I tapped my fingers against the side of my glass, barely able to hear the tinkle of metal on glass as my ring-covered hand beat a steady rhythm.

I only wish we knew, my grandmother sent, her amusement gone, irritation and worry replacing it.

"You're not hungry, my Ruler?" I turned my head, concentration broken, fixing my gaze on Elphremantic. While he appeared open and genuinely curious, I'd learned such an expression on the face of a demon usually meant I was about to suffer an attack of some kind.

"I am not," I said, sharply, on purpose, voice rising. "It is impossible to enjoy a meal under such conditions."

A few of the demons noticed, seemed to pay attention to my disfavor. But, within seconds, they returned to their ridiculousness and I could only flare my nostrils in annoyance.

"Perhaps a more private dinner would suit you," Elphremantic said. "Where you would have a better opportunity to get to know each of your suitors without being subject to," he looked around as though disgusted himself, shrinking back from the demon next to him when the bigger male slammed backward, catching a loaf of bread in one hand like a human football, "such distractions."

"On the contrary," I said, allowing my lids to fall half-closed, feeling my lips pull sideways, thinning my mouth. "This is precisely what I need to observe in order to make my choice. I can see now, very clearly," I gestured with my fork for emphasis, "none of those gathered here will ever be suitable choices for my mate."

I spoke softly this time. After all, this was a subterfuge and it was better to continue and gain some breathing space than to declare the fact none of the demons my grandfather presented would be coming anywhere near me anytime soon.

"I would hope," Elphremantic said, leaning slightly forward, "your present immediate company would be excepted from that statement."

How bold, Sequoia sent. *And yet, he appears at least marginally civilized.*

I took a sip of wine as I considered what to say to him. He didn't stand a chance, the poor boy. I'd already made up my mind. But he could be part of the illusion and cultivating a relationship with him might serve me well.

"Of course," I said finally. Elphremantic smiled, saluted me with his glass.

"Then perhaps that private dinner might not be a terrible suggestion?" His eyes glowed over the rim of his goblet.

"Perhaps," I said. "Tell me of your involvement in my father's enrichment program."

Elphremantic leaned forward again, face open and full of delight. "It was wonderful," he said, enthusiasm on the surface. "Your father was a wonderful Ruler, with a scope of vision few understand or appreciate." I didn't comment. Doing so would have been inappropriate, considering I still raged against Dad for his choices. "I grew up here, in Ostrogotho, pampered, to a life of privilege." He glanced sideways at the party going on, disgust clear on his face. "I was like them, once. But seeing how other demons live, how other cities are run, was an eye-opening experience. I understand how important good rule is, how vital our connection not just to the royal class but to all demons. Demonicon has been stagnant for centuries. Your father brought about change unlike anything that's happened to demons before." He could say that again. "In doing so, he's stirred inconveniences, I admit." My free hand clenched in my lap as I thought of the last four years and tried to fit them into the word "inconvenient" with no luck. "But I can see the vision of the future your father held, Ruler. And it is incredible."

I sat back, doing my best to contain my temper, forcing myself to process what he had to say. Could it be I had clung to the old ways out of habit, born from Ahbi's presence and, because of that, unwilling to see where Dad intended Demonicon's development to go?

Foolishness, Ahbi snarled.

There are many ways to look at an issue, Sequoia sent carefully. *It might be a good idea to speak with Elphremantic further at this point. Since change is now inevitable, having his insight and enthusiasm to draw on may make your life easier.*

I nodded, more to my friend than to Elphremantic, but he took it as an affirmation of his words.

"Ruler," he said, hand reaching forward to touch mine where my fingers clenched my glass. "I can only imagine how hard it is for you, despite your great power and brilliance." Only the flattery kept me from losing my temper, though I knew the reaction came from Ahbi. I could feel our separation now and wondered as he went on how much of my agony in the last four years came from her. If I had been alone in my head, would I have found things had gone differently?

"Go on," I said as I realized he was waiting for permission to continue.

"You are in an incredible position," he said. "To enact change and guide us into greatness, greatness that has only been potential since the joining of the planes.

Our first Ruler intended far more for us. But the restrictions required to maintain order ensured our stagnation."

"You seem to be very familiar with our history," I said.

He bowed his head. "Since Teris Haralthazar took power and I joined the enrichment program, I have made it my duty to educate myself on the policies, laws and past of our people. And the things I've uncovered have astounded and excited me. But more, they've convinced me we have so much further to go." Elphremantic's hand fell away from mine, a small smile increasing his handsomeness. "And you, my Ruler, are the perfect one to guide us."

How flattering, Ahbi snapped.

We've been working under the premise these changes were a disadvantage, Sequoia sent softly. *But what if Elphremantic is correct, my Ruler? What if we are intended for more but have never been able to break past our restrictive society to reach the potential inside us?*

Harry was a fool, Ahbi's anger made my skin itch as her power heated up, *and you two are bigger fools for listening to this young idiot.* I felt her turn away, cutting me off and let her go. If nothing else, Elphremantic had given me something to think about.

I drew a breath to comment, but a flicker of motion from the corner of my eye caught my attention first. I glanced at the exit, my gaze settling on a familiar face, filled with concern and anxiety.

Ram. I reached for him, Elphremantic and Dad and the evolution of demonkind forgotten, my relief at his appearance shutting out everything else.

Ruler, he sent. *I have to talk to you. And it can't wait.*

He disappeared back the way he came while my heart clenched in fear. If Ram was worried, we were in serious trouble.

chapter eleven

I closed my office door behind me, striding swiftly down the three steps and across the stone floor to where Ram waited. I knew Henemordonin would find time to personally chastise me for leaving dinner so abruptly, but I couldn't care less what he wanted and actually welcomed the confrontation for once.

Sequoia hurried along at my side, Jabut sealing the door with power before joining us. Pagomaris stood next to my desk, wringing her hands as Ram uncrossed his arms from over his wide chest and bowed to me.

"Ruler," he said. "I'm sorry to intrude on your dinner." His tone was lighter than it had been when he appeared at the dining room door, but I could still see the tightness around his eyes, the way his muscles bunched and shifted under the thin fabric of his white shirt, all signs of stress.

105

"Thanks for the rescue," I said, mouth as dry as my words as I went on. "Now, tell me what you found out that's so important it couldn't wait until the pack of idiots I just left nectared themselves into stupidity."

Ram's façade of cocky calm cracked. He ran one hand through his hair, and only then did I notice his right horn was scuffed, as though he'd been in a fight. Immediate worry for his well- being pushed me forward, my fingers slipping over the rough patch as he spoke. We were so close, my face just below his, I inhaled his breath as he answered me.

"We all scoffed at the possibility," he said, the rumbling of his voice making my skin vibrate. "Demons are the most anti-organized religious race the Creator ever conceived."

"And yet?" Sequoia's soft voice broke through the private bubble holding Ram and I, though she didn't shatter it.

His eyes left mine a moment, glancing over my head before lowering to meet my gaze once again. "Ruler," he said, "you have an infestation of religion in the outer planes. And it's spreading rapidly."

Cold fingers traced light patterns over my skin as goosebumps rose to attention. "This is insane." Where had the abrupt about face come from? What kind of religion could lure selfish and self-serving demons into its folds?

"The followers call themselves the Planeless," Ram said. "And those who convert to it do so quickly, with little convincing."

"Magic?" I stepped back from him. "It has to be some kind of coercion."

He shook his head, anger appearing, more out of frustration than real temper. "There is nothing," he said. "No hint of power being used." His amber eyes fired as he dropped his hands to his sides. "I have no explanation for you."

"What is their mandate?" Bless Sequoia for stepping forward while my mind churned. I could feel Ahbi listening, though she had as yet to contribute. I just hoped she'd stop sulking over Elphremantic's conversation and see this was more important.

I'm not sulking, she sent. *Now listen to the boy.*

Ram's shoulders twitched. "Mandate." His lips worked around the word as though it gave him pain to speak it. "Peace," he said. "Harmony. Kindness." He looked stunned, almost amused. "While on the surface such a goal is perhaps enviable, it's oddly repulsive in action." He shuddered visibly, rubbing his hands together. "But there's more. And this is the part worrying me the most." Ram sat on the edge of my desk, fingers gripping the edge tightly as he leaned back. "The converted are powerless."

Now that is a problem, Ahbi sent, tone so sharp I

winced from it.

"Powerless how?" I shoved her back and focused on Ram. "Are they being stripped?" If so, not only was it illegal to strip demons without trial, their pretense of preaching peace and demonly love was nothing but a lie.

A fake religion with power hunger behind it? That I would buy.

"Not at all," Ram said, shattering my attempt at understanding. "It's the most baffling bit in this whole situation. The demons in question give up their magic willingly, without a fight, and without becoming empty shells in the end." Normally, if a demon was stripped of their magic, they reverted at best to a child-like state and at worst into a mere empty husk.

"How is this possible?" I knew I sounded like a dumbstruck girl, because I felt like one.

"I don't know," Ram said, his grim words buzzing with power. "As soon as I understood what was happening, I returned immediately. But, Ruler, more investigation is necessary now the rumors have been confirmed."

"If they are giving of their power willingly," Sequoia said, tiny fingers tapping her chin as her little brow furrowed, "it's possible they are avoiding being emptied through acceptance. Consider," she dropped her hand, her agile mind hurrying her normally choice words, "the reason demons become a mere shell upon the loss of their power comes, not from the loss itself, but from the fight damaging some vital part of them."

"I'm not willing to test your theory," I said, "but it sounds logical." About as logical as any of this.

"Whoever is behind it," Ram said, "has the advantage of not only creating a willing group of followers, but has been, I can only guess, accumulating their power along the way."

Ahbi writhed inside me. *Thief!*

"We need to find their leader," I said while real fear—not the nebulous worry I'd been feeling, but the genuine, gut-wrenching article—ached in the center of my chest. "And put a stop to this."

"I've attempted to do so," Ram said. "The followers of the Planeless way guard their leader carefully. I'm baffled by the fact I've been unable to track him—or her—through magical means. There is simply no trail to find." His face crumpled a moment before he shook his head.

Chill daggers of pain joined the ball of fear in my heart. "No trail," I said, lips barely moving as my breath caught and my mind went places I didn't expect it to go. "The Brotherhood."

It was a short leap to Syd's old foes. The dark sorcerers of her plane hid themselves behind the emptiness of their magic. Though we thought them defeated, was it possible they somehow still had influence? I certainly wouldn't put it past them. And the similarity to the subtlety of this Planeless cult—I could think of it as nothing but—certainly felt like something the Brotherhood would do.

Ahbi grunted, as though I'd struck her with my words while Ram looked suddenly startled. *Impossible*, my grandmother sent. *They are human, mortals of your mother's plane. There are no Brotherhood sorcerers here. No sorcerers, for that matter.*

I believed her. But a tiny part of me held the terror close. "You know to whom I refer?"

Ram nodded slowly, breath coming a little fast. "I do," he said.

"Is it possible those of the Brotherhood were able to cross to Demonicon?" Their sorcery was undetectable by normal magical means. Which made them an immediate choice of threat, even as I scoffed at the possibility.

Ram didn't answer, frowning at the floor.

"I need to know." I touched his arm, his face rising, gaze locking with mine.

He reached back, squeezing my hand. "My Ruler," he said. "You shall have your answers." Ram's face tightened into resolve before softening as he released my hand. "I'll leave at once."

"Not alone." I spun and gestured to Jabut. My guard captain stepped immediately forward and saluted. "I want the two of you to be careful," I said, heart pounding for them both, though I was willing to admit my concern lay closer to my heart with Rameranselot. "Report back at least every twelve hours. And, under no circumstances, engage the Planeless unless you absolutely have to."

Ram's scowl preceded a quickly drawn breath. I didn't allow him to argue.

"Please," I said. "Ram, please."

He released his inhale and nodded. I watched as Jabut joined him, the two striding to the large window at the far end of my office, stepping out into the waiting transport that rose to greet them.

It can't be the Brotherhood, Ahbi sent.

I took some comfort from her insistence, thinking of Syd and wondering if I should involve my sister. But how could I bring this to Syd, without any kind of proof? Besides, Ahbi's words left me with a gaping question.

If not, then who? And what—for I couldn't bring myself to believe the company line of peace and love—was their ultimate aim?

I paced the halls outside my bedchamber as the evening turned into the darkest hours of the night. No amount of reassurance from Sequoia or Pagomaris could ease my troubled mind, and Ahbi's stubborn resistance to anything regarding the discussion I'd had with Elphremantic only made things more complicated.

My grandmother retreated from me again once Ram

and Jabut left, refusing to talk about the possibilities. Time with only my own mind for company was a rarity, and I welcomed the respite. Yes, she was still there with me, and I knew she would hear what I was thinking if she focused, but it was as close to being alone as I had been in years and accepted it with a breath of relief.

The only unfortunate part of being alone in my own thoughts was I had no one to work out issues with. I grew up as part of a powerful coven, though segregated slightly because of my visible heritage and overlooked often due to the rise and dominance of my very powerful sister. I had Sassafras, of course, to lean on and talk with, but even he was far too busy with more important things in the last few years I spent in Wilding Springs to have time for me. Bitterness lingered, though I did my best to heal it. The needs of a girl were far outstripped by the risks to an entire plane. I knew this in my heart. I grew up understanding responsibility and commitment to family were of the utmost importance.

Just for once, I would have loved it if someone put me first.

I looked down at my still feet, realizing I'd come to a halt while I wallowed in self-pity and prodded myself into movement again. Old hurts wouldn't help me now. I accepted this position knowing full well it would mean being on my own, without support. Only now was I realizing I craved what Syd had. Except I would never gain her position, not only because I wasn't maji, one of the oldest races, as she was, but because I chose to be Ruler to a race who would never support me the way the coven did her.

I shook my head at my own defeatism, biting my lower lip while my bare feet made soft slapping sounds on the cold stone floor. The quiet pressed in around me, only faint light warming the air of the hall, the odd guard at attention more like furniture than living, breathing demons. I did have support. I was beginning to gather more to me, in fact. Pagomaris with her steadfast and unconditional loyalty, for one. Sequoia and her soft advice, for another. Jabuticabron may not have been a friend, if only because he wouldn't unbend enough to allow friendship, but his commitment was never in question. And Ram.

I thought of Elphremantic, then, of his enthusiasm and faith in me I worried was unfounded. He might make a new addition to my collection of support. Henemordonin's attempt to marry me off might have succeeded in creating a firmer foundation for me to work from. The idea his own desires might serve me in the end made me laugh out loud.

My moment of jocularity was broken as a shadowy form detached from the darkness of a doorway and came to a halt before me.

chapter twelve

I drew a sharp breath at the sight, cutting off my amusement. Power crackled forth to protect me, a net of shielding flaring to life. The magic of Demonicon snaked out and sniffed at the energy of the demon standing before me. I allowed it to drop away, though I held my shields in place as I recognized the figure waiting for me.

I saw little of Bakari. My grandfather's private bodyguard stayed out of sight most of the time, though the few instances we did interact always left me feeling wary and out of sorts. I came to a halt several feet from the silent demon and crossed my arms over my chest, if only to hide the fact my hands were suddenly shaking. Bakari made me decidedly nervous.

"Ruler." He bowed his head, if barely. Bakari was one of the only demons who refused to genuflect properly, but I had never attempted to correct him. There was a cold calculation to him, more of a watchfulness, a coiling power that always gave me the impression he was far more dangerous than I would ever be. Pointing out his failings just didn't seem worth it.

"Bakari." Of course, he didn't need to know how I felt. I kept my tone cold and crisp, feeling Ahbi return and focus on the conversation.

Ask him what he wants, she sent.

I ignored her and chose my own words. "You can tell Henemordonin your attempt at spying on me for his pleasure is unacceptable."

Bakari's head tilted to one side. His long, black hair braided tightly into a coil, though less for fashion and more for practicality I guessed. He wore simple black leather, the vest over his chest open to show the lean muscles, a tight band gripping one bicep. I think it was his unadorned carelessness, how he seemed to look down on the rest of us that made me the most uncomfortable.

"I am here of my own free will, Ruler," he said, subtle chiding in his words.

"You are my grandfather's creature," I said, dropping pretense. I was tired of being afraid of him. "Don't try to convince me otherwise."

I had never heard him laugh, not in all the years I'd been here. It was a rough sound, harsh despite his cultured voice. I waited out his humor, waffling back and forth in fear and frustration until he shook his head, body relaxing from his typical ready-for-action pose.

"I fear you misinterpret our association," he said. "And the reason for my attendance on the Second Seat."

Interesting, Ahbi sent before I could speak in anger.

"Tell me, then," she said through my lips. "Why are you with him?"

Bakari shrugged, elegant and graceful, leather creaking ever-so-softly. "I'm concerned," he said. "Henemordonin has been a powerful voice in Demoniconian politics for many centuries, but he has seemed content to be the rebel, to work behind the scenes in opposing Ahbi. Even his climb to Second Seat was punctuated with his need to appear as a force for good while he undermines you in subtlety."

I gaped at him, unable to speak, and even Ahbi held her breath.

"In the past few years, he has changed," Bakari said, a tiny frown pulling his smooth brow forward. "He seems to be shifting his approach, something I honestly considered an impossibility."

"Old demons and new tricks," Ahbi and I said together in one breath.

"It is so," Bakari said with a tiny smile. So much approval from a demon I always thought was on the wrong side. It chilled me rather than warmed my heart.

"Why are you telling me this?" I forced myself to drop my arms, my hands falling to my sides though my toes curled under the hem of my dressing gown, my thick black nails scraping over the stone.

Bakari's expression smoothed to flat and cold once more. "First and foremost, my order is tasked to protect Demonicon," he said. "Our failure at capturing Ameline Benoit when she attempted to destroy the Node is a black mark on our history." Bakari's scowl was sharp and instant, flashing away as quickly as it came. "Your sister I found endlessly frustrating as she blocked my attempts to do my job. I thought it wise to approach you directly to prevent such an occurrence repeating itself."

Back to Syd again, only this time I almost laughed. I could tell, though, he respected her, and I could only hope he felt the same about me to some extent. It was only then I actually registered what he said, and realized I knew far too little about his particular sect for my liking.

"This order of yours," I said. "Who exactly are they?" I knew he was part of a special group of demons, though I hadn't gone much further in my investigation.

Assassins, Ahbi sent. *Spies. They have existed for far longer than I was Ruler.*

Bakari ignored my question as he asked one of his own. "You are currently pursuing the Planeless?"

My shields tightened in response. "You've been eavesdropping on me, I take it." I half turned, ready to call the guards. But Bakari raised one hand, a small gesture that caught and held my attention.

117

"Ruler," he said. "I mean you no harm. For as long as you work toward the health and prosperity of Demonicon, we are on the same side. I have been keeping up on your progress and wish to offer my assistance."

Can we trust him? I reached for Ahbi who sighed.

I don't know, she sent. *I just don't know.*

Being Ruler meant taking calculated risks. As I looked into Bakari's eyes, I chose to trust him, at least in part.

"I have sent two of my people to investigate," I said. "If you have helpful information, I'll make sure they receive it."

"My own people are looking into the matter," Bakari said, as though he were Ruler of his own little kingdom. "I promise you, when we know anything of value, we will share it. I am merely here to warn you of Henemordonin's shift in focus." He turned away before pausing and looking back, real concern on his face. "We are unhappy with the way things are evolving," he said. "And though we know change is inevitable, we must protect Demonicon at all costs."

"And if I go against what you and your order believe to be in this plane's best interest?" I already knew what he was going to say, but having him lay it all out for me could give me some perspective.

"You don't want to do that, Ruler," he said, ever so softly. "You really don't."

"And you might want to reconsider your tone," I said, just as softly. "You don't rule Demonicon, Bakari. Nor do your people."

He didn't move for a long moment. When he finally bowed his head to me, I allowed him a short, sharp nod of my own.

I let him go, watched him fade back into the shadows before turning toward my quarters to wake Pagomaris to dress me. My morning was going to start a little early today.

I had a great deal of research to do.

As I rounded the corner, head down, deep in thought, I only had a moment to realize someone waited for me at my door, flanked by two very stern-looking guards. Jabuticabron must have put the fear of his considerable power into them because they glowered and hovered over my visitor as though ready to tear him limb from limb.

To Elphremantic's credit, he seemed cool and collected under their scrutiny, a small smile on his handsome face. I slowed my approach, my frown of concentration easing as I neared him. He had a way about him that put me at ease, a kindness rare in demons. He reminded me so much of me when I first came to Demonicon, a sense of kinship arose and softened me toward him no matter my plans to use him to my advantage.

Who knew? Maybe he would see our association in

the same vein and be all right with our friendship.

"My Ruler." He bowed deeply to me, taking my hand gently in his before kissing my knuckles with his warm lips. "Forgive the early visit, but I wanted to check in with you and make sure everything was all right."

Ahbi crackled her dislike. *As if we need anyone to check in on us.*

I sighed at her. *He's just being nice*, I sent. *And obviously looking for a chance to talk to me. What's wrong with that?*

She fell silent as Elphremantic watched me with soft expectation.

"I'm sorry," he said, releasing my hand, "it's very forward of me to think you, of all demons, would need someone to ask after you. But you left dinner so abruptly and in some distress. I hope I haven't offended, my Ruler."

There, see? I shoved Ahbi's continuing grumbling aside as I allowed my frown to fade the rest of the way.

"Unnecessary," I said, "but appreciated."

He bobbed a quick nod as my guards backed off, returning to their statue-like poses beside my door.

"I can only imagine how taxing your position can be," he said. "I learned much in Bilhaeder, but only a fraction of what you endure on a daily basis."

Flatterer, Ahbi sent.

I knew it was exactly that. But who was to say I couldn't enjoy a little flattery now and then as long as I didn't let it get to me?

Exactly that, my grandmother grumbled.

"The weight of being Ruler isn't for the faint of heart," I said.

Elphremantic's horns glistened as he shook his head with a soft laugh. "Droll and charming. Excellent qualities in the finest Ruler I'm sure Demonicon will ever know."

I almost laughed, finding it incredibly difficult to hold in the burst of humor as Ahbi gasped and spluttered in my head.

I don't like him already, she sent.

Funny, I sent back as I felt myself warm to the cleft in his chin, the way his lean body filled out his clothing, how his amber eyes sparkled when he smiled. *I'm rather enjoying him.*

She didn't bother to say anything and that only made my need to laugh grow.

"I do have an ulterior motive for being here." Elphremantic's cheeks pinked past the red glow of his natural skin tone.

"I guessed as much." Actually, I hadn't, but Ahbi taught me being all knowing and all seeing—at least, pretending to be—was part of the mystique of being Ruler and I wasn't about to allow that particular painted backdrop to fall into misuse on my watch.

His teeth flashed white against his lips. "I had wished that was the case," he said. "I hope you don't think me overbold when I say the majority of the males you have at your disposal are unsuitable to the task of being your mate and Second Seat."

Blunt. Ahbi's irritation was finally getting to me.

Honest, I sent. "I noticed as much," I said.

"And while I would never assume, my Ruler," he bowed to me again, "I would ask you take my bid to join you as your consort into careful consideration. While we might not know each other well yet," the stress he put on the word "yet" actually made me inwardly giggly, "it is my hope you will come to adore me as much as I already adore you."

Well now, I sent to Ahbi. *How charming.*

She held her peace.

It helped, of course, I actually found him attractive. My smile came easily, my eyebrow arching before I could stop it, all the while I thought of Ram and how much I wished I could simply tell this demon I'd made my choice already.

"May I say," I leaned forward and touched the back of his right hand with my fingertips, "you are at the top of my very short list."

Elphremantic winked. "I'm honored."

"You should be." I stepped back again, gesturing at my door. "And now, if you don't mind, I'd like to retire."

He bowed one last time, stepping back as he did. "My Ruler," he said. "I look forward to our next meeting." I watched him go as he saluted and spun, gliding away, his lean body swaying on thin hips over a rather attractive backside.

Eye candy aside, Ahbi snapped, *you really need to learn to be more careful.*

My good mood shattered, I turned and entered my room, firmly closing the door behind me before answering her.

I believe you agreed to our little plan, I sent as I made my way across the main room of my quarters to my dressing chamber.

In theory, she sent. *But I can feel what you're feeling, Meira. Don't for a moment think I'm not aware of the fact you like him for real and not just as a smokescreen for what's really important.*

Excuse me for wanting to have a life, I snapped as I jerked loose my robe and tossed it aside. *I think I've earned the chance to do things my way, Grandmother.*

She huffed a moment before backing down. *I'm just saying, you need to be cautious. We know nothing of this young demon.*

I sank to the padded bench at the far end of the room and hugged my knees to my chest, looking out the one-way window over the dark city, the faintest light of the first sun's rise glowing in the east.

Centuries of being forced to watch your own back have made you cynical, I sent. *And untrusting. Yes, I know*, I stopped her in mid-interruption and forged on, *I know these are demons*

I'm dealing with, not humans. But I think you forget, while we as a race are driven by power, we are also capable of so much more. Sequoia is proof of that, as is Rameranselot. And Sassafras. I could name many more, your own son among them. She made a "pffft" sound in my head, though her tense anger faded to sullen acceptance. *Just please allow me to handle this. I'm not an idiot, despite what you might think.*

You know I don't consider you that way, she sent. *And you're right about me. Still, there is something about that young demon I mistrust.*

I'll keep that in mind, I sent, rising to my feet with a deep inhale. *But, for now, I'm going to allow him to court me if only to satisfy Henemordonin and the family I'm making progress in my selection.* I paused a moment, fingers deep in a cloak of fur so thick and soft I pulled it to me to stroke over my cheek. *Speaking of untrustworthy, I take it you have information about Bakari and his people you've failed to share up to this point.* I had to admit to myself it wasn't all her fault. I hadn't pursued the important details I should have and knew the failing was mine alone.

At this juncture, however, I wasn't beyond making her take on her share of the guilt.

Assassins and spies, she sent, *as I said. They have been around since the planes were joined, from what I've been told. And they live outside our laws, though many Rulers have tried to change that.*

You included, I take it? I released the soft fur and

stepped away.

I was never granted an audience with their leader, she sent, her unhappiness almost petulant. *And any attempt I made to do so by force was met with disaster. They simply vanish into thin air and are untraceable. Most frustrating. And my greatest failure as Ruler.*

My bare feet slid over the plush carpet beneath me, one hand sliding over the hanging costumes lining both walls. *That must have driven you to distraction.*

You could say that. Finally, some humor returned to her, though she sighed at last. *I did speak to Bakari many times about it, and his predecessor. But I always had the impression he worked in aid of Henemordonin, considering he left the Seat when I kicked your grandfather from the throne and divorced him.*

A logical assumption. But Bakari seems to think otherwise. I stopped at the end of the row of fanciful clothing and spun around, fingers tapping my lips as I considered the implications. *If Bakari isn't working for Henemordonin,* I sent, *what is the alternative?*

He's watching him, my grandmother sent.

Exactly. I chewed my lower lip. *Which means this sect of assassins and spies he claims are tasked with protecting Demonicon at all costs don't trust my grandfather.*

Ahbi fell still. *Meira,* she whispered, *if they haven't trusted him all along...*

What can he possibly be up to now that has driven them to warn me? I shivered though the room's temperature

125

remained comfortable.

Something even they have been unable to uncover, Ahbi sent.

Which means, I sent, *it's a warning I need to take very much to heart.*

I wished she disputed my conclusion. It didn't exactly improve my confidence level knowing she thought I was right.

chapter thirteen

Pagomaris appeared as though by magic as I turned to summon her. I had no idea how she was so able to assess exactly what I needed and when and simply took her almost paranormal ability to see to my every need as one of those things.

As she and her people worked hard to make me presentable, I reached for Rameranselot, hoping for an early update, but was unable to reach him. My inability to then connect with Jabuticabron only increased my nervousness until I became snappish and short with the demon maidens who attended me.

Pagomaris's soothing voice and gentle but firm demeanor helped me to relax to the point I apologized to her after the minions fled.

"Not at all, Ruler," she said over a curtsy. "You have heavy responsibilities on your mind we could not begin to fathom or bear the weight of ourselves. It is, instead, our happy duty to serve you, who serves us so faithfully."

I've never really been impulsive, more thoughtful to Syd's reactionary nature. But when instinct drove me to hug my aide, I obeyed, careful not to poke her eyes out with the spiked shoulder pads she'd added to my ensemble. I wasn't expecting her to hug me back, knowing how powerful her hero worship was for the First Seat, but she did, and, to my shock, she began to cry.

"I never tell you how much I appreciate you," I said. "But I really do."

She pulled away after a soft kiss to my cheek, dabbing at her eyes where tears glistened.

"My Ruler," she said, voice throbbing with emotion. "I live but to serve you, forever and always. It is my utter joy and my life's purpose, and I can only hope you will never find another who cares for you better."

I shook my head, the tinkle of crystals and gold pieces strung in my piled hair vibrating against my horns as I did. "Never," I said.

She bowed her way out as I pondered such loyalty and whether I really deserved it.

Such thoughts carried me to breakfast where a quiet Sequoia waited for me. When I had to frown the negative to her hopeful expression, she simply returned her focus to her meal, though I noticed she ate about as much as I did.

Pagomaris was exceedingly attentive as I rose to go to court and I realized our conversation only more firmly cemented her feelings toward me.

There's nothing wrong with that, Ahbi sent as I stepped onto the elevator and rose to the throne room at the top of the Seat. *In a world where most of the populace either resents you for your power or would sell their soul to have your position, a little undying dedication from your underlings is a rare and precious commodity.*

Pagomaris is not a commodity. I couldn't hold back the frost in my tone. *Nor would I ever take advantage of her loyalty in any way.*

I didn't suggest you would, Ahbi sent. *But, to be blunt, my granddaughter, your supporters are few and far between and there may come a time sacrificing one of them for the good of Demonicon might be your only option.*

What an excellent way to start my day.

My gaze settled on Bakari, hovering behind the Second Seat and my glowering grandfather, but the assassin's face was as silent and brooding as usual. I ignored him and Henemordonin, though I did spare the briefest of nods for Elphremantic who had carved himself a position near the front of the pack. From what I understood, placement in court was hard won, each small square of real estate flanking the center aisle fought over and coveted on a regular basis. I had to wonder how many demons he'd battled to win his way to the front and center, directly on my right side at the foot of the dais. The idea heated my blood somewhat, burning away my temper as I considered he'd fought for a place near me.

Ahbi's sigh of annoyance killed my return to positive attitude.

To my surprise and relief, court was moderately tolerable that morning, and when I called for the end to the session, Henemordonin didn't argue or bring up any conflict to the contrary. Feeling as though I'd somehow sidestepped a charging bull for the moment, happy to have come out of a whole three hours with my family unscathed for once, I was in a much better mood when I retired to my quarters for lunch.

Pagomaris was in the middle of serving me when one of her maidens appeared, head down, hands clenched before her.

"Your forgiveness, great Ruler," the girl said in a quivering voice, "but the Eighth Lady Zinniaperimote would like to join you for your repast."

The very fact Dad's ex-fiancé wanted anything to do with me made my eyebrows shoot up. He'd been forced to choose a consort and she had been his final selection. I still remembered our weekly chats, orchestrated by her, naturally, talks filled with discussions about hair and fabrics and absolutely nothing to do with politics. Back when I was only heir, I had the time to treat her with good will and more than a little sympathy. She was the kind of demon I wondered about, how she ever made it to such a high level plane when it was obvious to me she lacked certain hungry skills required to maintain her place. I had always guessed it was her disarming charm that kept her safe and unmolested by the others at court, though the fact truly baffled me.

Once Dad abdicated, her position as soon-to-be mate of Ruler vanished. I winced as I thought back to the moment she ran, sobbing, from the throne room as Dad handed over the power of Demonicon to me. I'd seen her a few times over the last few years, but she'd held back, stayed clear, and I was grateful. I had no idea how to treat her and didn't want to be cruel, though how could I possibly show compassion to a demon who almost took my mother's place?

"My Ruler," Pagomaris said. "Your decision?"

She's harmless, I said to myself.

Nothing and no one is as they seem, Ahbi sent. *You might want to find out what she has to say.*

I gestured to Pagomaris. "Bring her in."

My mind whirled in chaos as I considered what Zinniaperimote might have to tell me. It could be she simply found her nerve at last, wanted to burn me with shame over my father's actions. But no, I couldn't bring myself to believe that and, when she appeared, dressed demurely with her hands folded before her, head slightly lowered, a worried frown on her face, I realized such thinking was uncalled for.

Zinniaperimote curtsied deeply to me, her thick skirting whispering its fabric song as she sank almost to the floor and rose again. "My Ruler," she said, voice low but clear. "My thanks for seeing me on such short notice."

"Please." I motioned for her to come closer as Pagomaris had two of her maidens set a second place at the small table. Ostrogotho stretched out on my left side, my seat next to the deck railing, looking down over the city. Zinniaperimote didn't glance at the view, simply slid with a nod of thanks into the chair beside me and raised her eyes to meet mine.

It took me some time to adjust to the fact all demons had amber eyes, so used to alternate colors in humans I found, at times, the lack of variety almost disconcerting. But, over time, I noticed variations in tone and pattern, color and depth, enough to create my own mental palate. Zinnia's were clear, almost crystalline, with only the faintest of tracking of a darker color around her curved iris, slightly cat-shaped. I found her gaze as transparent as her eye color and felt myself retreat from her as she leaned forward, concern on her beautiful face.

"I have a matter of utmost urgency to bring to your attention," she said, voice barely above a whisper. "I would have sent warning through a servant, but I believe the threat to be imminent."

Interesting, Ahbi sent. *I always thought Zinnia uninterested in politics.*

"Go on," I said.

"Lady Tanasharia and several of her associates," Zinniaperimote's voice rose and fell with disdain, "are plotting against you as we speak."

"Hardly shocking," I said, swirling my *vrena* as I silently cursed my cousin and wished Syd and Dad had allowed me to strip her power years ago when I had the chance. "I'm sure I'll survive this latest attempt at humiliation."

Zinniaperimote's thick hair brushed over the table cloth as she came closer still, eyes earnest and power tightly contained. I would have felt threatened if she didn't feel so worried for me.

"This goes beyond some mere attempt to undermine your power, Ruler," Zinniaperimote said. "From what I know, she is planning to challenge you for First Seat."

She'll fail, Ahbi sent with firm conviction.

As long as she doesn't cheat, I sent, not so confident. "Thank you for your warning," I said. "Considering our background, it's generous of you to make the effort."

Dad's former fiancé sat back, eyes tight. "I mean no offence to you or to Teris Haralthazar," she said, "but your father's laws are most troublesome. Anyone can challenge to be Ruler now, and I'm quite shocked no one has attempted it yet."

Ahbi bristled at her forwardness, but I kept control.

"While I agree with you the new laws have forced change," I said, letting Zinniaperimote feel my disapproval, "I am in complete control, thank you. And can take things from here."

She paled slightly before rising and curtsying again. "Forgive me, Ruler," she said.

I waved her off, but spoke as she turned to go. "Really, my dear," I said in my best Ahbi voice, "what makes you think I haven't already successfully crushed all opposition? Or that I didn't know of Tanasharia's ridiculous little plan?"

Zinniaperimote didn't comment, though, for a moment, her face betrayed her disbelief. But when she rose from a final curtsy, she offered a tiny smile.

"I have absolute faith in you, my Ruler," she said. "I only wished to show my loyalty. Sides will be chosen in the days ahead and I wanted you to know upon whose I reside."

I let her go as Ahbi hummed monotone.

Pagomaris came to my side, her anger clear on her face. "My Ruler? Shall I have Lady Tanasharia arrested?"

I smiled at her and patted her hand. "Not yet," I said. "But please inform the Guard to keep a close eye on her the next few days and alert me of whom she talks to."

My aide bowed herself out as I turned and looked

over the city.

I actually hate to agree with Zinniaperimote, Ahbi sent, *but I'm surprised, as she is, no one has attempted to usurp you.* She sounded as puzzled as I now felt.

Maybe Henemordonin has been protecting me from some twisted sense of need, I sent. *Better the young demon Ruler you know?*

Which means he's now removing his protections, you're thinking? Ahbi shifted inside me. *So his push to have you mate is part of a subterfuge, the means to lull you into assuming your position is secure.*

You certainly do see shadows behind every door, I sent.

Experience, she snapped.

I agree with you, I sent, sad as I looked over my city. *We already know he's a master manipulator. And that he would never willingly give up power. Which means your conspiracy theory is likely on the right track.*

So what do we plan to do about it? Ahbi's coldness sent shivers from my insides out.

We plan to crush him like an insect, I sent, casual and equally chill. *Will that suit you, Grandmother?*

Completely, Granddaughter, she sent.

How lovely to know we were both on the same page when it came to Henemordonin and his demise if he came against us.

The trick will be linking him to Tanasharia, Ahbi sent.

You're far more clever than he is, I sent. *I'm sure together we'll come up with something.*

Sequoia slipped silently to my side, taking the seat Zinnia previously occupied, so swift and quiet I jumped when I caught her settling out of the corner of my eye, breaking my concentration.

"Ruler," she said with a tiny smile. "Forgive the interruption, but I thought you might like some good news." Her dimples deepened. "A message from Lord Theridialis. If you have time, my father would like to see you."

chapter fourteen

The moment my feet touched down on the stone hall leading to Theridialis's tower, I breathed a sigh of relief, welcoming the smile and warm feeling spreading through me, growing more powerful and cathartic with every step. Sequoia, normally one step behind me, kept pace at my side, her answering grin a mirror image to mine.

Her father didn't await us at the platform where I left the guards. Nor did he come for us at all. Instead, Sequoia and I traversed the length of the hall, my gaze drifting over the large balcony overlooking the city as we passed, my focus shifting back toward the door to Theridialis's extensive laboratory.

We found him hunched over a set of beakers, humming off key to himself while he dripped tiny amounts of a glowing blue liquid into each of them. My entire being relaxed as little puffs of smoke emerged from the line of vials, some squeaking in a tiny voice, others bursting with rainbow light. The last one let out a giant boom so loud I jumped, almost missing the soft belch at the very end.

Theridialis sat back with a delighted expression, thick hands patting the roundness of his belly as he turned toward us. Joy lit his eyes, his pudgy face lighting with it as he held out his arms to us both.

"Dear girls," he said, gesturing for us to come to his side, "how lovely to see you."

Sequoia kissed her father's cheek as I hugged him and did the same to the opposite side, the warmth of his skin under my lips and the scent of chocolate and cinnamon hearts waking the happy girl inside me.

He hugged us back before releasing us, beaming smile shining. "How lucky am I to have such delightful visitors."

Sequoia laughed and patted his hand. "Father," she said, "you're so forgetful when you're working. You asked us to come, remember?"

I would have worried, except his daughter was right. I'd often spent hours watching him work, waiting for him to notice me after he'd asked me to come visit. I never complained, though. There was such a lovely feeling to the old scientist that brought me out of my Ruler persona and back into plain old Meems. It was nice to spend a little while pretending, especially since his genuine nature shone through in everything he did. In fact, I don't think he ever once called me Ruler.

I loved him for that.

Theridialis's face crumpled into a thoughtful frown a moment before he shook his head and laughed. "It will come to me," he said as he rose to his feet, round belly swaying as he waddled past us with a gentle squeeze to my hand. "Come, sit and keep an old demon company while he tries to remember why he asked you here."

I joined Theridialis and Sequoia at a small table under a large window. His tower reached far into the sky, though no match for the height of the Seat. I actually preferred his view, the closeness of the city, the way I felt as though I were part of it instead of being so far above and out of touch.

My father's oldest friend reached for a steaming jug, pouring out a cup of nectar. The scent reached my nostrils, making my senses flare and the old addiction rise. A flash of Sekaniphestat's face crossed my mind as Theridialis filled a second mug. But when he moved to pour a third, Sequoia's hand covered the lip, a frown tightening her brow.

"Father," she said.

He tilted his head to one side before paling, setting the jug aside. Theridialis engulfed one of my hands in his with a sad scowl. "Meira, my dear, forgive an ancient fool."

I managed a smile, one of many I'd forced to my lips in situations just like this. "It's fine," I said, even though I knew it really wasn't.

It would never be fine, thanks to his dead wife. Her plan to control me, using her adapted nectar to speed up my development and addict me to her brand of nectar, ruined me forever. Even now, as he turned from me and lifted the mug to his lips, my mouth burst with saliva, the need for the flavor of the nectar so great I could taste it in the back of my throat. My body begged for the chocolate deliciousness, for the burst of power promised in its depths. There was a time I avoided nectar altogether, only to realize that strategy merely put me at a disadvantage. The first time Henemordonin drank a cup next to me at a court dinner, eyes locked on mine the entire time while Ahbi held down my writhing soul, I knew I had to find a way to desensitize myself from the burning need.

It took a few months to be able to sit still without Ahbi's help. And now, years later, I could observe with some detachment despite my body's urgent desperation.

I wish I could have shielded you from what she did, Ahbi sent, tone sad and deep.

We've had this conversation, I sent as flares of memory rose—

I ache all over, screaming as Sekaniphestat stands over me, glowing eyes cold and calculating—

Hot nectar pours down my throat, burning a path through my system, my power flaring from contact even as my soul shrivels—

I'm in a fog, the world around me distorted and webbed with cracks around the edges as I speak through my lips, though the words aren't my own, fury and hate aimed at my sister who stands in a dark cavern, staring up at me in shock and horror—

Child. I snapped out of the cycle, the sky suddenly too bright, the chair I sat on hard-edged and painful. My eyes fell to my hands, half way across the table, reaching for the nectar while Sequoia and Theridialis stared.

I'm okay, I sent to Ahbi as I firmly tucked my hands back in my lap. "I need to be exposed," I said, keeping my tone firm and level. "It's fine."

I'm tired of hearing you say that, Ahbi sent.

Best I can do, I'm afraid, I sent back.

Theridialis set his mug aside, sadness suddenly altering into a light-bulb moment as he snapped his fingers. "Nectar!"

"Yes, Father," Sequoia said, worried eyes never leaving me. "Though I disagree with Ruler's choice to torture herself so."

He shook his head, bald pate shiny in the light of the suns pouring through the window. "My darling daughter," he said, "nectar is the reason I asked you here."

Wild hope surged in my chest, radiating outward as I leaned toward him. "You've found a cure?" He'd been searching for years for the means to clear my system of the addiction.

His face fell yet again as he sighed. "No, I'm afraid not," he said. "But I do have something to show you." Theridialis lurched to his feet, crossing the room to retrieve a flask which he brought back to me. My eyes locked on the deep indigo liquid as he offered it to me. Sequoia tried to block him, but I seized the canister before she could, and she backed off with a small nod of apology.

"This is nectar?" I sniffed it, grapes and what smelled like peanut butter calling me to chug the liquid PB&J. My hand shook slightly but I was proud of my ability to give it back to him without submitting to my craving.

"It is," he said, sitting again, swirling the purple stuff around inside the vial. "As you know, there are many different kinds of nectar." I knew that, intimately to my great regret. "Most are power inducers," he gestured at the mug beside him, "a mild stimulant. Others are more intense and bring about rigorous response." Firsthand knowledge of such concoctions almost dragged me into memory again. Only Ahbi held me firmly in place and I silently thanked her for it while Theridialis went on. "This particular blend is new," he said, his round face now pinched with curiosity mixed with concern. Knowing Theridialis treated everything with the child-like innocence of a true scientist, for the pure knowing of things, the fact he seemed worried troubled me deeply.

"How so, Father?" Sequoia took the vial from him, sniffed the top, examined it as she held the deep fluid up to the light. Purple sparkled in a prism across the back of my hand as the suns diffused the nectar and sent beams of color around the room.

"Rather than boosting power," he said, tapping his thick fingers on the edge of the table, "it contains a mild suppressant. It serves to soften the edges of magic, to soothe the monster within." I shivered at the reference. "I'd heard of it, naturally. But this is the first sample I've been able to get my hands on."

"That makes little sense," Sequoia said, setting the vial down on the table. I swallowed hard, averting my eyes, keeping them locked on the bald scientist so my addiction riddled mind wouldn't fixate. "Demons crave power, not the other way around."

Theridialis stared out the window a moment, and when he spoke his words were soft, thoughtful. "Demon youngsters are using it in growing numbers," he said. "Because the blunting of their magic is a novelty. They then engage in battles for power that amount to little more than giggling matches." He shrugged, smiled as he turned back to us. "Harmless, and yet, curious. Why anyone would consider creating this type of nectar in the first place has me baffled."

Ahbi hissed in my head. *The Planeless.*

I'm sorry, I missed your mental leap, I sent. *What about them?*

Meira, child, think. She shuddered within. *The demons who are converting are powerless, correct?*

That was what Ram said. I suppressed my own shudder as the implications became clear. *You think a stronger version of this could be the method the Planeless use on their followers?*

Ask him. She mentally tapped her foot. *Just ask him.*

"Theridialis," I said, leaning forward as Ahbi stewed, "have you heard of the Planeless?"

Sequoia gasped, covering her mouth with her hands as her father shook his head.

It took only a moment to tell him everything I knew. Theridialis leaned back as Sequoia stared at the vial of nectar as though it were about to bite her. "Fascinating," he said. "And entirely possible. This is a mild version of what could very well be the controlling substance you would need to negate the power of demons."

"Which means they could still have their power," I said. "Rather than it being drained from them, it's only being suppressed." That did make me feel better. If so, whoever was leading the cult wouldn't be all-powerful after all.

If, Ahbi sent.

"Sickening," Sequoia whispered, wide eyes meeting mine. "The demons who are converting likely have no idea they are being controlled in the first place."

"I also detected a coercive in the nectar," Theridialis

said, now sounding as troubled as I felt. "Again, a stronger version could easily supplant the will of the demon drinking it, making him or her susceptible to suggestion."

"Maybe this is how they first introduce the cult," I said. "Beginning with the young demons in each city, supplying them with this mild version. Then, when the Planeless begin actively recruiting, it only takes a dose or two of the real thing to suck them in."

Ahbi's anger snapped and popped. *Insidious and brilliant*, she sent. *And absolutely unacceptable.*

"Theridialis," I couldn't help the snarl of anger accompanying my words, "is there a way to reverse it?"

He shrugged, fingers sliding over the glass vial. "Possibly," he said, "though I would need a sample of the full dose nectar to find an antidote." He held up one hand. "If there really is such a nectar. We are only working on supposition."

I stood abruptly, nodding. "Time to find out," I said. "And the elements help whoever it is because, if they are drugging my people, I'm going to eat them alive."

chapter fifteen

I disembarked from the transport, still fuming over the thought nectar was the source of my worries yet again. Sequoia hissed softly at me as I looked up and realized we weren't alone.

Normally, I would have ridden my transport right to my quarters, but I knew I had to find Henemordonin and talk to him about this. While he may not have been on my side, the health and well-being of our citizens was at stake, and it was time I filled him in on what I knew.

I shouldn't have been shocked to encounter resistance. Sequoia logged our flight return, so the appearance of Tanasharia and her gathering of not-so-bright minds waiting for me at the far end of the transport bay was irritating, but not all that shocking.

How fun to simply crush them all and toss them over the side, I sent to Ahbi. *Do you think we could get away with it?*

Worth a try, she growled. And sighed. *Oh for the days such an act was possible.*

I didn't doubt she, at the height of her power, would have been able to get away with mass murder. I was sure if Ahbi wanted Tanasharia dead, the girl would have met an untimely and likely messy end with not one scrap of evidence connecting my grandmother to her death.

We'll talk, Ahbi sent.

"Ruler," Sequoia spoke softly. "We can return to the transport and have it deliver you to your rooms after all."

"And back down from them?" I glared as Tanasharia and her friends laughed and made a general spectacle of themselves, fully blocking the exit from the bay. "Never. Not a chance in hell. Wild drach could not drag me away."

Sequoia snorted a laugh. "Nice to see you in such fine spirits."

"Let's kick some demon butt," I said, grinning at the thought of Syd and how I wished she was there to help. We'd had some fun together our first visit to Demonicon before things became so complicated, and I found the idea of going to battle at my sister's side again oddly appealing.

Head up, face fixed in an angry grin, I stormed the distance between the transport I'd just left and the exit, maintaining my speed even as I drew close to the gathering. They tightened ranks with whispers and laughter, though a few grew concerned as I continued my charge, especially when I allowed them to see, with a ripple of sparks, the thick shields I'd built before me. The wedge-shaped prow of my wards super-charged with magic, crackling and flaring while my grin widened and my speed increased.

Tanasharia's anger visibly flared as her gathered supporters scattered with cries of fear, falling back from my advance to hover and watch. I allowed my protections to retreat, no longer extending out in front of me, merely coating me with glittering amber fire. I glared at my cousin without a word, glad now Pagomaris chose my chrome platform boots that morning as they gave me a solid three inches over my scowling relative.

She leaned in, shoving a silver flask toward me, her knuckles skimming over the surface of my shield. "Nectar?" I drew a quick breath, the scent of peanut butter and jelly strong as she exhaled all over me.

Under normal circumstances, I would have been all right, quite able to cope with the enticement. But I'd just spent the last hour or so talking about, remembering, breathing in the scent of nectar and this final assault almost did me in.

A roar of hate leaves my mouth, power sizzling in eagerness to crush the dark-haired human woman staring up at me, magic howling while my soul screams in torment—

Ahbi's mind snapped across mine just as something

hit Tanasharia's hand, knocking the silver flask out of her grip. It spun in sparkling circles, crashing to the floor before spinning under a transport and grinding to a halt. I looked up from my cousin's sullen eyes to find Elph—the pet term seemed to suit him now—standing over her, body shaking with what I could only guess was rage. My dazed state held me hostage as his magic flared and lashed outward once again. The few demons of my cousin's entourage who remained groaned and collapsed to their knees as my rescuer's magic crushed them slowly to the ground.

"Show your Ruler respect," he snapped. "Before she orders you stripped and killed for such impertinence."

"She can't," Tanasharia said, eyes narrowing as they fixed on me. "Thanks to Daddy dear. Isn't that right, Meira?" She drew out the "e" sound in my name with a snarl in her voice.

Do something, Ahbi barked just as Tanasharia howled in pain and collapsed on the stone. Sequoia rushed forward, tiny body quivering, both hands glowing with amber fire.

"Incorrect," she said. "Nor does she need to act herself, in this instance. One more word from you and I shall kill you myself."

My cousin crawled away on her belly, fury in her eyes though she didn't fight back. Ahbi prodded me forward, my self-possession returning as I brushed past the still-groaning demons and out of their presence.

Cool air hit me in the face as I passed through the exit and into the stone hall on the other side. Four guards snapped to attention, two of whom looked suddenly guilty.

"Jabuticabron will hear of this," Sequoia snapped at them. "Your disloyalty to Ruler shall be noted and dealt with."

All four looked suddenly ill before bowing deeply to me. I ignored them, shoving them back with magic to crash into the walls where they remained until I rounded the corner and released them.

"My apologies, Ruler," Sequoia said, voice shaking. "The Guards are my responsibility while my brother is gone." I didn't know that. How was it I remained unaware of the workings of my own people? "I will see to it they are punished."

"Leave it," I said, tired and shaken, more from Tanasharia's open challenge than anything. "At least now we know Zinnia's warning was accurate."

Sequoia hissed a breath as I turned and realized Elph was still with us. Rather than try to hide what I'd just said, I offered my hand which he took with great aplomb. "Thank you for your timely interjection," I said. "Though unnecessary, such support is rare and welcome."

"Ruler," he said, kissing the back of my hand, "such support shouldn't be necessary. But is it my great honor to serve you in all things." He released his grip on me, lips still tight with anger. "Even in Bilhaeder I heard of how you were ill used by Sekaniphestat and forced to ingest nectar of her creation." His amber eyes flashed. "Your endurance and perseverance in the face of such torture is legendary and I can only express my absolute awe at your ability and strength."

He likes to talk, Ahbi sent, but her tone was thoughtful rather than sarcastic for once.

"Might I say," he leaned closer, "in light of everything you have had to face, as a demon princess, heir, and now as our beloved Ruler, I think you are the most amazing person I've ever met."

His lips met my cheek for an instant, the heat of his breath stirring across my ear before he pulled away, head ducking.

"Forgive my boldness," he said before saluting and bowing one last time. "Always at your service." I watched him stride off while Sequoia took my hand and squeezed it.

"How delightful," she said.

Isn't he, though? Ahbi fell silent as I turned and headed for the elevator, frazzled, but grateful I had a new friend to count on.

chapter sixteen

I remained sunk in whirling thoughts mixed with nectar need, the Planeless, my cousin's boldness and the image of Elph's smiling face when I entered my private quarters to the sound of arguing.

Pagomaris spun as I crossed the threshold, Sequoia falling behind me, my aide's face dark red with anger. She dipped a deep curtsy while Henemordonin, his large bulk dominating the room and, from the looks of things, trying to bully Pagomaris, loomed and scowled.

"Ruler," my aide said in a voice shaking with emotion. "Forgive me, but he would not leave when requested."

"I am Second Seat," he roared at her as she cowered briefly, but refused to give ground. "You do not order me."

I was used to him yelling and had spent years learning to fear it when he raised his voice to me. But so much had happened between the last time he managed to corner me and make me feel tiny and this moment I was a very different demon. A very different Ruler. And no one—no one—treated my friends that way.

With a roar of my own, I pinned my grandfather with the power of Demonicon. It rushed forth with eager vengeance, lifting him bodily from the floor and slamming him down again so he was forced to one knee. My need to hurt Tanasharia translated into my attack on Henemordonin and the rational part of me knew it. Even so, I was done and finished with being treated like his subordinate instead of the other way around.

I think I actually frightened him. At least, he didn't immediately lose his temper and come after me. Instead, he stared, mouth open, eyes full of shock as I pushed harder, Ahbi supporting me fully while the magic of all planes snarled and crushed my grandfather under its weight.

"You dare." I turned his words back on him. "Don't you ever, ever, talk to her that way again. For that matter," I jerked on the power holding him down, tightening it like I'd lassoed a bull, "the next time you speak to me that way, I'll take your head from your shoulders and have it for dinner." His mouth snapped shut, anger showing up in a rush of blood to his face. Ahbi held him silent while I battered him with magic. "The law might keep me from killing you outright, but you have invaded my personal space for the last time. Know this: you are Second Seat because I allow it. Laws or no laws, Henemordonin, if you come against me I will destroy you."

He pushed himself against me, trying to rise. I held him in place, grinning as I had in the transport bay, showing my teeth and my intent.

"You did your best to teach me to fear you, to control me," I snarled over him, "took advantage of a young Ruler who didn't know better and had yet to find her feet." My shoulders straightened as I allowed my upper lip to curl with contempt as he knelt there before me, fighting with all his strength, strength that would never be enough. "You've proven your disloyalty and manipulations often enough. It's time you understood I will no longer stand for any of it."

"Release me at once." His words gasped from his constricted chest as his lips turned purple from lack of oxygen.

"Tell me you didn't just give your Ruler an order." I sent fire through the power holding him, watched him writhe in pain before dampening the flames. "You will ask. Nicely."

Ahbi's laughter was tinged with hysteria. *Child*, she sent. *Oh, child.*

His nostrils flared, power dimming in his eyes as he poured everything he had into one final push against me.

I slammed him hard, sending him to his hands and knees where he panted short, almost impossible breaths.

"Apologize," I said in an airy voice, examining my fingernails, frowning over a chip in one. "Pagomaris, fetch the file. I appear to have broken a nail."

Henemordonin collapsed on his face into the plush carpet. "Forgive me," he whispered. "My Ruler."

Well, I'll be a charbroiled drach, Ahbi sent.

"I didn't hear you," I said, prodding Henemordonin with one chrome toe.

You're making an open enemy of him, my grandmother sent.

Good, I sent, my calm almost cracking as my built-up years of anger tried to take over and just kill him already. *It's time things were clear between us.*

"I beg you," he choked, "release me, Ruler."

I let him lie there another moment, heard his ribs groan as I pressed just that much harder before relinquishing my hold all at once. Henemordonin heaved a massive breath of air, panting into the carpet while I stood over him, hands on my hips.

He slowly leveraged himself up, face masked into cold fury as he straightened to his full height and did his best to dominate the space yet again with his bulk. Before he could succeed, I placed a ceiling of power at his shoulders and pressed down again.

"Now," I said, "if there's nothing further, get the hell

out of my quarters."

Henemordonin glared at me, his power building yet again.

"Is this the moment?" Ahbi spoke through my lips, quiet, deadly. "Is this the time you come against us and commit yourself, Henemordonin? Are you prepared for the outcome?"

He froze, magic build coming to an abrupt halt.

We waited, silent, at the ready until he finally backed down, bowing his head to me.

He brushed past me, his departure abrupt and swift. But as he reached the door, his arrogance returned.

"You are as unpredictable as your dangerous sister," he snapped. "Reckless and putting all of us at risk with your deplorable temper."

Hadn't the coven once believed that of Syd? I laughed in his face, tapping him firmly in the chest with Demonicon's eager magic.

"Get out," I said, still laughing. "And watch your back, Grandfather."

His final act of defiance was the door slamming behind him.

Pagomaris instantly fell to her knees at my feet, clutching my hand in hers, pressing it to her cheek as she wept. "Forgive me," she said, hoarse as she sobbed. "I never meant to be the cause of such strife."

I pulled her to her feet, Sequoia helping me guide my

aide to the window seat.

"It's been a long time coming," I said. "Thank you for a very satisfying few minutes."

She wiped at her eyes, black makeup tracking down her cheeks. "Ruler, I beg you, take caution. He will destroy you if he can."

That's hardly in question, Ahbi sent, dry and with a measure of her own satisfaction. *At least you've stood your ground. He'll think twice before pushing you around again. But, she's correct in her assessment. We've made him more dangerous as he will now be forced to work behind the scenes to destroy you.*

Something you have a great deal of experience with, I sent. *I'm not worried. We can handle him. It's the rest of this mess I'm more concerned about.*

Ahbi's power perked a moment later as the veil hummed. I reached for the mind on the other side, still keyed up and prepared for anything only to feel a familiar and well-loved presence poke me.

I can only assume your enthusiasm involves me, Sassafras sent in his dry tone.

I gasped and held onto him as the tear in the veil widened and his fluffy white form appeared in the gloomy basement on the other side. "Sassafras!"

He licked one paw several times before setting it back down in the nest of his soft tail encircling him. "Meira," he said. "Just saying hello."

The sight of him made me want to weep openly and

hug him tight. "Can you come visit a moment?" I held out my arms to him, amazed they shook as the aftereffects of my battle with Henemordonin finally caught up with me.

"Since you asked so nicely." He hopped through the veil in a rush of silver fur, flashing across the barrier and into my arms. I cuddled him to my chest, turning to sink down onto the window seat Pagomaris rapidly vacated to give me space. Sass's purr rumbled against me, his power spreading out with its soothing comfort. I'd recognized since I was a child how he manipulated all of us with that purr of his, but I, for one, welcomed it, knowing it came from his absolute love for me.

"It's so good to see you." My words barely left my lips, a struggle to speak past the thickness of my throat, my eyes burning with the need to shed tears.

"You, too," he whispered in my ear as his tongue swept across my cheek. "I hoped to speak to you at your birthday party, but you weren't in a state to hear me. Were you?"

I shook my head, felt Sequoia and Pagomaris retreat, giving us privacy as I snuggled my oldest friend and did my very best to keep myself from falling into pathetic pieces of demon girl.

"Something's changed, at least, according to Syd." Sassafras patted at me with one soft paw. "I wanted to see for myself if you'd finally come to some sense."

the planeless

Smart-mouthed cat, Ahbi sent to both of us.

Arrogant old biddy, he responded crisply. *Have you been tormenting my poor Meira?*

Not I, she sent.

It's all right, I told my demon cat. *I've worked some things out in the last few days. I'm sorry I've been so distant.*

You know I'm always here for you. Sass's mental voice was as sad as it was quiet. *You've only ever had to ask. But I knew you would find your way, Meira. You were always the more logical and practical of the two.*

I'm not sure those are the traits I wish I had, I sent, releasing him enough to kiss him on the forehead. His purr intensified.

They are for the task you've chosen, he sent. *Syd would never have been able to take First Seat. Demonicon would have been in flames long before now.*

Thanks for the vote of confidence, I sent. *But there's still time for fire and destruction.*

His eyes narrowed, tail thrashing once against my side. *I take it there are details I'm missing.*

You could say that. I sighed and stroked his fur, from the top of his fuzzy head to the tip of his thick tail. *Oh, Sass, I think I've made a right mess of things.*

I doubt that, he sent. *But perhaps you could use an extra set of paws right about now?*

The little girl who lived in me squealed in excitement though I did my best to hide her enthusiasm. *The kids*, I sent. *Gabriel and Ethie are your responsibility now, Sass.*

Ridiculous, he sent, swiping at me with his claws out, the sharp tips sliding over the slick leather of my bodice. *Not only are those two guarded by the dumb dog*, I grinned at his mention of the Wild Hunt hound, Galleytrot, *but they have the entire coven and two very powerful parents watching over them. Not to mention a pair of sorcerers.* Gram and Demetrius had to be home in Wilding Springs, then. *Besides*, he head-butted me, *you will always be my responsibility. And no matter how big you get, how old you grow, you will always be my little Meems.*

There was no way to contain the single tear that escaped to trickle down my cheek and I didn't try. He stood on his hind legs, paws on my shoulders, and rubbed his furry face against the moisture, soft and cool.

Thank you, I sent. *I could really use your help right now.*

Then it's decided, he sent. *Close that thing and fetch me a pillow. I need a napping place.*

I laughed, gesturing at the veil which snapped shut behind him, the fact he'd ordered the leader of all Demonicon to serve him not lost on me in the least.

I was about to rise and do exactly as he wanted—of course I was, this was Sassafras, after all—when the window behind me shuddered and a transport slammed into the wall beside it. I leaped to my feet, power crackling around Sassafras and I, my shields blocking off the window as he hissed in my arms, only to realize we weren't under attack.

Quite to the contrary. I took one look at Jabuticabron's distress as he hovered on the transport and dropped my shielding, opening the way through the window as well. My guard captain staggered through the gap, falling heavily on the window seat, amber eyes meeting mine, full of fear.

I could think of only one question to ask him as my own anxiety spiked abruptly.

"Jabuticabron," I heard myself wail his name, "where is Rameranselot?"

CHAPTER SEVENTEEN

Sequoia rushed forward, bending to help her brother sit up as my guard captain caught his breath.

"My Ruler," he said in his deep voice, "he's joined the Planeless."

I gaped, heart stopping in place as Sequoia shook her head far more firmly than necessary.

"Impossible," she said, glancing my way while Jabuticabron sagged, face falling in exhaustion. "He would never do such a thing."

"And yet, he did, sister," Jabut said. His broad face wrinkled in frustration. "We are in serious trouble, Ruler."

Sassafras wriggled in my arms until I put him down. He waddled to the bench and hopped up, climbing into Jabut's lap. "Tell us everything," he said.

The large guard stroked the cat's silver fur gently.

"There's little to tell, brother," he said. "We left here directly with the plan to scout a large group of Planeless gathering past Nunaresh." The outlier's city wasn't aligned with any planes, so I supposed such a location for their meeting was the most logical. "I've never seen so many demons gathered in one place." He swallowed hard, hands clutching at Sassafras as his eyes locked on me. "Ruler, they chanted a name over and over, a mass of demons so large and diverse in plane power I worry they've emptied many of the outer planes already of their inhabitants."

Though of limited power, the residents of the outer planes nonetheless fed the Node and kept those areas in balance and connected to the rest of us.

"Go on," I said.

"When he appeared, they all bowed to him," Jabut said, an air of awe in his voice. "He told them to rise, that their days of bowing were over."

"What did they call him?" Sassafras's crispness seemed to cut through his brother's moment of shock.

"Xeoniteridone," Jabut whispered. "He was… my Ruler, he was nothing short of magnificent."

It was difficult to contain my irritation at such a response, not to mention my worry over such a clear and blatant attempt to control my population. "What did Ram do, Jabut?"

The large guard nodded swiftly, drawing a steadying

breath. "It was his plan to infiltrate the cult," he said. "I did my best to attempt to convince him otherwise, but he insisted the only way to uncover the truth was to join the Planeless and see its power structure from the inside."

The young fool, Ahbi sighed.

"Knowing full well he'd lose access to his power," I snapped, anger fed by fear rising to the surface and taking control of me. I allowed its dominance. I would need such to keep me from going after Ram and personally wringing his neck.

"Brother," Sequoia said, "answer me this. Were the cult members drinking nectar?"

Jabuticabron frowned before nodding slowly. "They were," he said. "Though like no nectar I've ever seen before."

I suppose we've answered that question then, Ahbi sent.

"Was it purple?" Sequoia met my eyes.

Jabut nodded again, sealing the deal as he looked back and forth between us with growing concern piled onto his already giant weight of worry. "What has happened?"

I stepped away, turning my back on them as Sequoia told her brother of their father's discovery. Ram's face swam in my mind, the need to know his fate burning holes in my patience until I turned back to the three siblings even as I reached out with the power of Demonicon and tried to find him.

My other attempts had been mostly half-hearted,

knowing he was meant to contact me and likely hid from outside contact as a protective measure. But this time I refused to hold back, sharply focused on finding and retrieving him while Jabuticabron went on with his story.

"We found nothing we could use, had no other way to uncover information," the guard captain said, his entire being begging me to forgive him. "Rameranselot ordered me to return here to you and tell you of his plans. But I remained and waited to see what would become of him. I couldn't simply abandon him to the Planeless in case his duplicity was uncovered."

Cold fingers of fear danced a soft pattering rhythm up my spine though my skin burned with a sudden sweat. "They found out he was spying."

Jabut's face twisted, the hulking guard so near to tears of his own I had to catch my breath in answer to his distress. "Ruler, they did not," he said. "There was no need. The moment he drank of the nectar, he was lost. I almost pulled him out then, but to do so would have exposed me to their power and I, too, would be gone." He hung his big head. "I would have gone with him, but my responsibility to you is more powerful than my loyalty to him." Jabut beat the side of his head with one fist in a burst of disgraced anger. "I don't deserve to continue serving you."

Sequoia caught his hand before he could hurt himself while I searched and hunted for any trace of Ram. "This is not your fault," she said, eyes pleading with me to speak up, to save her brother from his shame. Ahbi's swift anger cracked my frozen soul.

He should be punished for abandoning his post, she snapped.

Shut up, Grandmother, I shot back as the power of Demonicon sniffed out the last trail of my demon friend and found it at last. I followed it swiftly along the path of where Ram had been, slamming with more force than I intended into a wall of darkness as the trail ended abruptly.

Something reached back. I flinched, Demonicon's magic fleeing from the emptiness as we retreated to the Seat with my heart pounding and the fear I knew who was behind this alive and well again.

"Meira." Sassafras leaped from his brother's lap and came to me. "What is it?"

I bent and lifted him into my arms yet again, hands shaking for a far different reason this time. "The Brotherhood," I said, the reminder of them fresh now I'd encountered this strange power. "We're certain they are destroyed?"

Sass snarled a whine of unhappiness before shuddering his cat body. "They are reduced to nothing," he said. "Why?"

I opened to him, allowed him to feel what I'd felt at the other end of Ram's trail. "It feels like sorcery," I said. "That emptiness is so familiar, isn't it?"

He was silent a moment before snorting. "There are no sorcerers here on Demonicon," he said with so much conviction I doubted what I'd felt immediately. He'd trained me well from childhood to accept what he said as truth. But I wasn't a little girl any longer and had been through enough trials on my own I pushed past my reaction and challenged him as I'd never done before.

"We're absolutely certain of that?" Even Ahbi felt hesitant though she had been as adamant as Sassafras was just now. I turned to Jabut. "When Ram drank the nectar, what happened to him?"

"I tried to maintain mental contact," Jabut said, misery coloring his voice, raising it until he sounded almost child-like. "But when he drank, it was as though a shutter closed around him, cutting him off from me. And the instant change in him, the way he looked at their leader..." Jabut shuddered. "I managed to pull him away from them for a moment, to see if he was simply acting the part. He turned them on me, my Ruler." Jabut shook, face crumpling as his lower lip trembled. "They surrounded me, attempted to force me to drink the nectar. Ram was in the forefront, encouraging me. I've never seen such fanaticism. It was no act, I swear it to you." He sagged against his much smaller sister. "I was fortunate enough to fight my way free, though it wasn't much of a fight, in all honesty. Their attempt to hold me down faded at serious resistance, declarations of peace and love falling from their lips like poison." Jabut's hands coiled in his lap as though he wished to strangle something or someone. "I was shocked they actually let me go, as though believing the propaganda they spewed. But Ram is one of them, now. And if someone like him can be so easily lost, I fear we are all at risk."

We all fell silent, Pagomaris huddled in the corner, staring with wide eyes as the rest of us fought with our thoughts.

"Let's say this is some kind of sorcery-based power," Sassafras said. "Where would it come from? In all the thousands of years Demonicon has existed, sorcery has never appeared."

"You're certain?" I hugged him in apology. "Of course you are. All right, then. That leaves an outside introduction. We've already seen two sorcerers come to Demonicon."

"Syd and Ameline don't precisely count," Sass said. "Your sister and her dead nemesis were both on the path to becoming maji at the time and had demon souls to help them cross over."

"So whoever this Xeoniteridone is," I said, "could he have come from Earth?"

Sass looked up at me, sparks flaring in his eyes. "Another demon hybrid child."

Ahbi grunted her disagreement. *The crossings of demon children from the other plane have been exceedingly rare. And not one of them had done so during my watch.*

Which leaves mine, I sent, including Sass in our private conversation. *Since this whole cult thing appears to be recent, could Xeoniteridone have crossed over in the last year or so?*

Possibly, Ahbi sent. *Though I'm certain we would have felt it.*

Unless he used sorcery to mask his crossing, Sass sent. *If that's the case, he could have come over at any time and your argument, Ahbi, is invalid.*

If the Brotherhood is involved, I sent, *we should tell Syd. This could mean they are gaining a foothold on Earth all over again.*

Sassafras's claws dug into my arm. *It is possible this is a coincidence as well,* he sent. *I know, I know, I don't really believe in them either. But there is a chance if it is a hybrid child with sorcery, he made his way here on his own.*

I really had to talk to Syd.

Regardless, Ahbi sent, *we now know we have a huge problem on our hands. We need a plan and the freedom to execute it.*

I groaned, thinking of the fight I just had with my Second Seat. *The likelihood of Henemordonin backing me on anything from now on is pretty much out the window.*

Not if he understands how important this is for the safety of Demonicon, Ahbi sent.

We'll see, I sent. I spun back and addressed the others. "Pagomaris," I said, "can you please fetch Jabuticabron a refreshment and something to eat." She flashed me a relieved smile, her servant's soul showing her gratitude for giving her something to do in this time of stress. My aide bobbed a fast curtsy before fleeing the room. "Sequoia," I set Sassafras down again, crossing to the window with swift steps, staring out at the distant tower were her father lived. "I'd like you to fetch your father. I want him working here, in the Seat, for the duration. Where I can get my hands on him when I need him."

She rose gracefully, tiny body tense but expression firm and sure. "I'll return presently," she said before hurrying out.

I finally sat next to Jabuticabron who focused his attention on his large hands, hands that shook as much as mine. I took one of them between my fingers and flooded him with the power of our planes.

"I'm so sorry, Ruler," he whispered, thick lips loose as he slumped forward. "I wish I had just killed their leader when I had the chance." He did look up at last, a giant of a demon reduced to misery. "For, I fear if something isn't done in short order, Xeoniteridone will have converted the entirety of Demonicon within the next few months, and there will be nothing we can do to stop him."

chapter eighteen

It would have been so easy to sink into his despair and allow myself to retreat. Or, perhaps, call for Henemordonin and lean on him, ask him to forgive me for thinking I could ever have filled this position when I really had no idea what I was doing or how to combat this threat to my people.

"Surely, it's not so bad," I said.

"If only that were true," Jabut said. "Ram and I traveled to many of the outlying planes, only to find them empty, their farms deserted, towns home only to the ghosts of their old inhabitants." His shoulders straightened somewhat as Sassafras hissed at his brother. "Forgive me, Ruler," he said. "We will, of course, do everything we can to stop the spread of this... disease." Both hands slapped down on his thighs. "I have faith, now you are aware of the problem, you will act with swift and decisive measures to put an end to the advance of the Planeless."

If only I could turn his words into confidence. "Have they penetrated the cities yet?"

"They have," he said. "Though in small numbers. It is my guess—and that of Rameranselot—their intent was to begin in a grassroots manner, gathering the weak-minded and less powerful to them as a basis of followers before attempting to bring their beliefs to larger, more influential populations."

"We need to know if they have come to Ostrogotho yet," I said, thinking of Theridialis and his suppositions about the weak form of nectar making the circuit. "Tell me, could this Xeoniteridone possess some kind of additional power he uses to convert his followers?"

Jabut nodded slowly. "I believe so," he said. "Despite my concerns about his people, his words were oddly compelling, as though he spoke to my very soul."

"Coercion," Sassafras said, tail snapping back and forth. "Despicable."

"But subtle," Jabut said. "I felt nothing of his influence even though both Rameranselot and I were hyper vigilant about power output."

"So some combination of the nectar to soften them up and suppress their power," I felt my hands tighten into fists in my lap without my permission, "followed by a coercive magic to capture and hold their weakened minds."

Sassafras growled.

"What does that get us?" He crouched, fur standing on end.

"A war we can't fight through normal means," I said. "Though perhaps a show of strength, at this point, might be the best choice."

I disagree, Ahbi sent. *Consider, if you will, a peaceful movement led by a charismatic leader being met by violence.*

This is Demonicon, I sent. *We're known for our violence.*

True, Sassafras sent. *And yet.*

You are already having trouble with your court, Ahbi sent, *thanks to Harry's meddling. It's possible demons such as Tanasharia and even Henemordonin might attempt to use such a salvo against a group intent on everyone just getting along as the means to show you as an unfit leader. While a show of power is acceptable, attacking those who are weaker than you, who offer no return violence, may be seen as you simply trying to retake the power over Demonicon you lost through Haralthazar's new demonocracy laws.*

I grumbled an agreement while Sassafras sighed.

I take it Harry's attempt to improve things has had the opposite effect?

How little he knew the truth of his words. *It doesn't matter now*, I sent. *Like it or not, I'm Ruler and the safety of Demonicon comes first. I'll just have to act and clean up the mess once this crisis is over.*

While attacking a bunch of helpless and powerless demons. We'll see how far you make it before your grandfather challenges you for real and has the court deem you unfit as Ruler. He won't have to fight you, Meira. Ahbi sighed. *He will simply take your power from you and have you imprisoned while the Planeless continue to depopulate the magic of the planes.* She shivered inside me. *As much as I despise the thought, demons are thinking differently, more in tune with your father's convictions. While I believe they have no place thinking they can rule themselves, the damage is done.*

Sassafras's mind hugged mine though I could still feel his concern through the curtain of comfort he offered. *There must be a way we can officially observe these cultists without starting a war. Your first task, Ruler, is to find out as much as you can about their leader without sacrificing more of your people.*

First hand, I sent, sharp and vicious. *Let him try to convert me.*

I don't know that's wise, Ahbi sent, but I was already standing, nodding to Jabuticabron as Pagomaris hurried back into the room, laden with a tray of food and drink.

"I've long planned a tour of the cities of Demonicon," I said. "My Second Seat has made it clear in the past such a tour is against his better judgment, but I'm thinking getting out and about would be an excellent idea."

Jabut rose to his feet and bowed to me. "As you wish, my Ruler," he said, though he sounded as if he wanted to argue with me.

I pressed my hand against his arm as Pagomaris set the small table, guiding the large demon to a seat while Sassafras leaped up onto the surface and helped himself to a bowl of milk.

"We need information," I said. "For all I know, at this point, the movement is genuine."

You really don't believe that, Ahbi sent.

Maybe not, I sent as Sassafras looked up from his drink, pink tongue sliding over his nose, *but it seems you've left me little choice but to observe the Planeless for myself.*

I agree, Sassafras sent. *And, if he proves to be a threat, we can make a plan to attempt an extraction.*

I nodded while Ahbi sighed.

Very well, she sent. *Though I suggest putting people in place now in preparation for that extraction?*

If Jabut is correct, I sent, *doing so will get us nowhere.* I thought of Ram and though I was still angry with him, my worry won the day.

We'll find him, Ahbi sent. *And we'll get to the bottom of this.*

I fully expected my grandfather to object and offer his usual arguments about such a tour of Demonicon, but as I braced myself for his typical opposition, my back rigid on my throne as the gathered court listened with barely contained excitement, I was shocked when he simply nodded.

"An excellent idea," he said, as though he'd never once told me I was foolish, childish, or irresponsible for wanting to visit each of the major cities of Demonicon.

I highly doubted the difference in his attitude was lost on the family, either, even though no one said anything against him, naturally. And, to be quite forthcoming, I was so surprised by his abrupt change of heart I didn't prod him as to why he'd decided all of a sudden my plan was a good one.

Will wonders never cease, Ahbi sent with a soft whistle.

"In fact," Henemordonin went on in his ponderous voice, turning to face the court as my moment of relief faded, "it's perfect timing for court to go on tour and observe first-hand the changes we've enacted thanks to the alterations in our laws. To see, with our own eyes and hear with our own ears how the demons of our plane are adjusting to the beginnings of our demonocracy."

Ahbi growled. *Just lovely*, she sent.

Henemordonin turned back to me, eyes full of quiet watchfulness. "What say you, Ruler?"

He has us cornered and he knows it, Ahbi sent. *Damn him to the depths of the Seat volcano and may his privates rot in a rash of nectar fever.*

It's a compromise, I sent.

It's a trap, she snarled.

I slowly nodded to my grandfather. "Very well."

If you don't figure out a way to put an end to him, Ahbi

grumbled as court burst into excited babblings, *I'm going to do it myself.*

What's the big deal? I didn't like the small smile Henemordonin wore, nor the sly look Tanasharia shot me. *We're accomplishing our goal—getting out there to see the Planeless, aren't we?*

You have never been part of a court tour, Ahbi sighed, her anger sagging finally. *Meira, this is a disaster.*

Two days and a circus of organization later and I had to agree with her. My intention to head out that very afternoon was immediately kyboshed when a slew of requests to accompany my retinue blew up from a handful of high-ranking demons to literally the entire membership of the court. And their children, servants, private guards, pets and the majority of their wardrobes.

I told you, Ahbi sent as I gaped at the growing pile of requests. *And you can't say no.*

I can't? I sat back, hand already aching though I had as yet to pick up my quill to begin signing them. *Why not?*

Because, silly child, Ahbi snapped, *you told Henemordonin you approved of his suggestion. Now you've saddled us with most of the major households down to the lowliest servant. And there's not one thing you can do about it.*

Doesn't that put the entire court at risk if something goes wrong? Surely, I could come up with a good reason to keep at least some of them home.

Ahbi's mental laughter made me scowl. *Not one of them,* she sent, *would willingly miss a second. There has never been—and will never be, I expect—any kind of restrictions on tours like this one. You're stuck with them, my girl.*

I couldn't resist coining a Syd. *Oh. My. Swearword.*

Though the "swearword" I replaced with something much more dramatic and shocking. My sister might have been a prude in certain ways, old fashioned in others, but I didn't have her reserve when it came to swearing. Living on Demonicon had taught me that much.

"We could just leave," I said as I paced my room that first night, Sequoia calmly weaving a tapestry with magic, the amber lines of her enchanted loom hovering in the air. "Call it an advanced party or something."

"Impossible," Pagomaris said, face paling as she waited with great impatience for Sequoia to finish what she was doing. "I have six more gowns to make before we go!"

I rolled my eyes at her. "This is a ruse, remember?" Her face fell, hands clenching together in front of her. I should have known better than to push my aide when it came to this kind of thing. "Pagomaris," I said as gently as I could, crossing to touch her shoulder while she bowed her head, "the gowns can wait."

She bobbed a nod and snuffled softly. "Forgive me," she whispered. "I forgot."

"That's it," I said, spinning to leave the room, "I'm

going, with or without all of you."

Jabuticabron stood before the door, shaking his head. "Ruler," he said, "you know I would be the first to follow you. But you've committed to this action. We must see it through."

"If you leave now," Sassafras said in her infuriatingly calm voice, "Henemordonin can challenge you for First Seat. Without you here to defend it, he could conceivably take over the throne without contest." He batted playfully at the threads his sister wove, tail twitching as his cat instincts took over.

"Well, that sucks," I said, sinking to a padded armchair, angrily crossing one leg over the other, my platform boot bobbing in time with my tapping fingertips. The soft fabric of the armrests crushed under my aggressive touch. "How long is this going to take?"

Until every single demon you so kindly welcomed to join us is ready to lumber their way across Demonicon, Ahbi sent.

I spent the next day signing more paperwork, arguing with rising heat against my advisors and worrying about Rameranselot. They had no idea I continued to search for him, though every time I encountered the dark magic, I shied from it, worried I might trigger some event I wasn't prepared as yet to tackle.

By the end of the second day, I was fully prepared to tear out my hair before murdering the next person who came into my office with a ridiculous request for me to sign.

"This might be an excellent time to contact your sister." Sassafras crouched on the corner of my desk, amber eyes following me as I paced the room. I felt much like a caged animal in a zoo, knowing I had to escape the Seat but trapped by my own idiocy.

"Syd, right." I'd been putting off getting in touch, not because I didn't want to see her, but out of worry involving her would mean this really was a Brotherhood initiative. Mind you, Sassafras had already talked to her about the situation, but bringing Syd in made it very real to me, and I had other things to worry about.

No, Ahbi sent as I reached for the veil, *you don't. You have many things to consider. You are Ruler and don't have the luxury to choose which situations get your attention.*

Thanks for the reminder, I shot at her as I felt Syd connect with me, the tear opening in the veil. Syd's answering scowl told me my expression wasn't exactly welcoming. She crossed from the dark basement and into my office, human form so small compared to me I immediately sank to the edge of my desk so we were at equal eye height.

The veil slipped closed behind her as my sister's magic rippled in iridescent waves around her.

"What's wrong?" I could feel her need to act, how wound up she was, and sighed, shaking my head.

"Nothing," I said, tapping my temple with one finger.

"Just having a conversation I'd rather not participate in."

Syd grinned, relaxing instantly. "Feel you," she said, crossing to me for a hug before scratching Sassafras behind the ears. When her blue eyes rose again to meet mine, she wasn't as grim as she'd been when she arrived, but she didn't look happy, either. "I hear you might have a Brotherhood infestation."

I laughed at that. "Worse than roaches."

She grinned again, arms crossing over her chest. "I've held off because Sass asked me to," she said. "But if it is the Brotherhood, I need to act, Meems."

"And doing so," Sass said, "could very well undermine your sister's place on the throne and give Henemordonin more ammunition in his attempt to gain further power and control."

Syd nodded, frowning over her suddenly flashing eyes. "I know that," she said. "I said I'd wait, didn't I?"

"And you have," he said. "We're only now preparing to depart."

"Tomorrow, hopefully." The sigh that left me sounded petulant to my ears. "I screwed up, Syd. The whole court is coming with me, all because I didn't know the rules." My head hung without my permission, eyes burning with the need to cry. Only a very tight hold on my power kept my cheeks dry.

"Meems," Syd's hand settled on my arm, "you don't have to apologize to me." I looked up as she gave me a rueful smile. "How many times did I make a ginormous mess?" She let her hand fall. "We'll—no, you'll—figure it out. And kick some Brotherhood butt."

"If it's the Brotherhood," Sass said. "I'm still not convinced." His silver fur shimmered as he licked one paw with vigor. "It's possible this Planeless cult has nothing to do with sorcery."

I opened to Syd and Sass both, allowed them to feel what I felt when I sought Ram. Syd hissed, Sass answering her with a snarl of his own.

"Holy," Syd said. "Feels like sorcery to me."

Sassafras nodded, a slow and reluctant motion, silver mane shuddering as he did. "Agreed."

"But still no proof of the Brotherhood," I said. "I'll keep you posted, but I think Sass is right about this. Let me investigate further. Once we know what we're dealing with, I'll publicly invite you to come and help. But until we have proof, it might be best to keep you out of it."

Syd's face flickered with concern. "Things that rocky here, sis?"

Emotion rose, choking me as I held her gaze. "You could say that," I said. "The last four years have been interesting. And if you want me on the First Seat for much longer, this is the best way to go." I stood, towering over her though, as always, she felt so much bigger than me, her maji power glowing around her. "I need to play Ruler," I said.

Play, Ahbi growled. *Is that what this is to you?*

You're the one who said this is a game, Syd's voice came through loud and clear. *If I recall correctly, Grandmother.*

Ahbi grumbled and retreated.

"It might be time for you to go it alone in more ways than one," Syd said, voice layered with meaning. "I know how hard it can be to balance more than one personality. But mine are all tied to my power. Yours has her own path to choose."

Why did the idea of losing Ahbi suddenly make me feel ill? It could have been my grandmother's influence, but I doubted it. I hugged myself, feeling the demon spirit living inside me perk and pay sullen attention as I answered.

"That time will come," I said. "But not today."

Syd nodded before stepping back. "If this isn't the Brotherhood," she said, reaching for the veil, "the implications of demons finding sorcery after all these centuries is massive, Meira."

"You don't have to tell me that," I said.

"I know," Syd said. "Love you."

"Love you, too," I said, waving as she crossed back to her plane, the veil snapping shut behind her.

chapter nineteen

"My Ruler," Pagomaris beamed a smile at me as she bowed while her minions dressed me the next morning. "Your caravan awaits you for departure."

"About damned time," I muttered, shooing off the three maiden demons who fussed over the hem of my heavy skirt. It clacked with irritating abruptness as the large panels of thick plastic they'd sewn into the seam swung and clanked against each other.

I glared at my aide who appeared instantly distressed.

"You don't like it," she said.

If anyone was ever closer to being yelled at… my temper had worn to a frayed edge and she was a convenient target. Only the sad look on her face kept me from screeching my irritation at Pagomaris for dressing me in the most inappropriate travel outfit I'd ever seen— or had the misfortune to wear, for that matter. A towering collar, higher than my impressively piled hair, dominated the gigantic shoulder plates and bulky wrist cuffs in a way I didn't think possible.

Ahbi sighed. *Let it go*, she sent.

You're kidding me, I snarled back. *I look ridiculous*. While I rarely argued with my aide over her choice of wardrobe, often enjoying the elaborate get-ups she came up with, I was in no mood to be a walking spectacle today.

"Take it off," I said, voice level and cold despite the desperate urge I felt to increase my volume by about a million decibels. "Now."

She pouted and complained with her expression, a true mistress of guilt, but this battle I would win.

By the time she had me stripped down to the thin leather body suit I'd worn under the giant contraption, Pagomaris wept softly. Sequoia quickly bundled her off, eyes widening at me as her jaw clenched, apparently blaming me for my aide's state.

I huffed myself down from the dressing platform, glaring until the maidens fled—within seconds, truth be told, their forced departure requiring little effort on my part. Impatience dominating my mind, I dove into my wardrobe and pulled free a thin, lace poncho. I loved it but had only worn it twice. Pagomaris hated when I repeated outfits, claiming it was my responsibility to set the stage for fashion on Demonicon.

You give her too much leeway, Ahbi sent as I slipped the

curtain of lace over my head, my hair making it almost impossible as the giant, three-hived wrap she'd made of my curls caught and pulled. *She's turned you into a doll to be played with and mocked.*

Grandmother, I sent as coldly as I could muster, sending a chill from my witch magic through the demon fire holding us together, *you can be a real bitch sometimes.*

Yes, dear, she sent.

I glanced in the mirror, aware there was nothing, at this point, I could do with my hair, though at least my attempt at dressing myself hadn't succeeded in ruining what Pagomaris created. I'd had enough of her tears without having to endure her huffing and sniffing over my head.

At least the sparkling wrap I now wore was more to my taste, the heavy lace falling to the floor around me in a drape of crystal-covered darkness. I slipped my hands through the subtly crafted sleeves hidden inside the drape, fingertips emerging through the surface.

It will do, Ahbi sent. *Now, shall we finally get this show on the road?*

My thoughts exactly, I sent.

I made it partway to the door when I realized my quarters weren't as empty as I first thought. Bakari stood by the window, watching me with his cold eyes. How had he made it past my guards? And had he watched me dress? My cheeks heated as I switched directions immediately, joining him as he turned to look down and out the window. I sighed, embarrassment fading, at the sight of what had to be a hundred transports, some small and sleek, others gigantic, loaded down with guards and trunks, packed with eager demons of lesser planes waiting for me.

"Any news?" I looked away, stomach churning at the thought of the swath we were about to make across Demonicon and hoping somehow this would all work out.

"Of the Planeless, no," he said. "Though I have spoken to the leaders of my order. They are concerned by my report and are willing to discuss tactics with you once they have investigated further."

How nice of them, Ahbi sent.

"I advise caution," I said, ignoring her dry sarcasm. "One of my own people fell victim to the cult after only the briefest of contact. The other barely escaped to tell me of his fate."

Bakari's amber eyes narrowed. His were very dark, deeper than most demons, filled with swirling black lines. "Who?"

"Rameranselot," I said as Bakari's face tightened with anger. "You know him?"

"You're certain he was not using subterfuge?" He always felt dangerous to me, but no more so than now, hovering over me with the threat of violence quivering in the air between us.

"Positive." Years spent trying to stand up to Henemordonin while he yelled at me served me in this instance, my voice level, though nothing could prepare me for Bakari's true anger. I was certain at any moment he would lash out and kill me with a single blow and not even the power of Demonicon would be able to save me.

He finally backed down, head swiveling abruptly as he stared out into the morning. "I will pass this information along," he said, his normally soft and crisp voice harsh. "We will take every precaution."

Bakari left me without another word, striding for the door which he closed firmly behind him. I stood there a long moment, breathing, just breathing, both hands pressed to my chest as my lungs and heart gradually slowed.

Still shaken, I left my quarters, almost running into Sequoia. She took one look at me and frowned, hand on my arm, but I shook my head and moved on, head high, reaching for the cloak that was Ruler while Ahbi hugged me.

Well done, she sent. *He scared me, too, you know.*

The elevator descended quickly, delivering me to the transport bay while I exhaled the last of my fright and strode with false confidence toward my personal craft. Jabuticabron stood next to it, gesturing with a sour expression toward one of the larger transports, already packed with chattering demons.

"My Ruler," he said. "Your court awaits you."

I came to a firm halt, scowling at him. "I'm taking my own craft," I said. "Stand aside."

Jabuticabron's face twitched as a shadow fell over us.

"Ruler," Henemordonin's huge hand landed on my shoulder, squeezing without a hint of gentleness. "Shall we?" He gestured at the big transport, eyes glowering, waiting for a fight.

Son of a... I let the swear trail off as Ahbi agreed, though with far more of an "I told you so" feeling to her than I liked.

The demons in my path parted rapidly as, still fuming, I stormed my way onto the full transport and, shields firmly creating a path, I forced my way to the front and sat without grace in the foremost seat, right hand side. Henemordonin took his ponderous time, greeting family as he went. I could hear him smooth-talking his way forward, refusing to participate as I glared out the softly tinted shielding now in place into the first three suns of morning. When he finally sat, the transport powered up. I would have preferred to control it myself, but that, too, was out of my hands as the four pilots seated behind us joined magicks and stirred the large carrier into motion.

A fanfare of blaring pipes, much like trumpets only sounding more of bagpipes with a chest cold, pealed out across the city as we soared forward. The curved surface of the bubble of power reflected back to me the long line of transports floating along behind us, an endless train of ridiculousness.

It was going to be a very long trip.

A furred body leaped into my lap, Sassafras's heavy weight settling down.

This is stupid, I sent.

Welcome to being Ruler, he sent as Ahbi laughed.

It's not as if you would have been able to sneak around anyway, she sent. *Even if you had known not to accept your grandfather's terms, either he would have found a way to delay you and come about to this result, or made sure every city on the planes knew you were coming.*

And isn't this the point? Sass's claws dug into my legs through the thin leather suit. *To give them a show while the rest of us do some investigating?*

I'm more curious why your grandfather didn't argue with you this time, Ahbi sent, suddenly sobering. I caught sight of him out of the corner of my eye. He was watching me and his intent attention made me nervous.

All part of his plan to get rid of me, I guess, I sent. *Why else?*

Ahbi didn't respond, but Sassafras did. *If you're worried, I'm worried. We'll keep an eye on him. In the meantime, we have to focus on the Planeless and hope whatever Henemordonin has cooking stays on the back burner until we can find out what's going on.*

I wasn't hopeful.

chapter twenty

Tanasharia's not-so-subtle jabs at me started up pretty much from the moment we took off. Nothing overtly vicious, mind you, but sharp enough I felt my shoulder blades wind tighter and tighter as her brazenness grew.

"I'm sure I'd never be able to carry off that hair style," she said from behind me. I refused to offer her the satisfaction of turning around to glare. "So... last century."

It didn't help her friends, seated with great enthusiasm right behind me, laughed at every nasty line.

Ignore her, Sassafras sent while my grandmother stewed with the need to slice the girl's head from her shoulders. And I thought Syd had a bad temper. She held nothing to Ahbi.

You ignore her, she sent. *I'm going to kill her.*

Now, Grandmother, I sent, welcoming the amusement

of the pair of them arguing. *Decorum. Above all else, Ruler must be an example to her people.*

Don't quote your grandfather's tripe to me, she snapped.

I smiled despite Tanasharia's continuing efforts to anger me. In fact, I smiled because of her. Bless Sass and Ahbi for putting everything into perspective. Tanasharia didn't matter, my cousin's attack a mere distraction. I was Ruler and she was nothing.

With a casual turn of my head, I leaned across the aisle and back to where Sequoia sat behind Henemordonin.

"The air is rank in here," I said, loudly enough everyone on the transport could hear. "And hot. Could you speak to the pilot, dear, and have them vent the source?"

Sequoia's eyes widened, her throat working a moment before she answered. "Yes, my Ruler," she said while moisture rose around the corners of her gaze. *Do not make me laugh*, she sent with a mental snort.

I leaned back, my own lips tight with a grin, my cousin's sudden silence and the brooding pressure against the back of my chair enough evidence my message made it through clearly. Now, if only I could actually vent her for real, this trip might not end up so badly after all.

Now who has a temper? Ahbi's smugness fed my own good humor.

If you two are done playing, Sass sent. *Really, Ahbi. You spent how many years trying to teach me to behave only to become a hoodlum yourself.*

Takes one, she sniffed.

Henemordonin's displeasure rolled from him in waves. But I had backup like never before and engulfed myself in Sassafras and my grandmother.

Nicely played, my Ruler. Elph's mental voice came through to me softly, hesitant, as though he was unsure of his welcome. I blushed instantly, heat rising from the pit of my stomach to light my cheeks. I was just grateful no one could see me.

No one but Sassafras, that was, and, from her vantage point inside me, my grandmother.

Interesting, Sass sent, having no compunctions about peeking around the edge of my chair, I could only guess with the goal of spotting my young demon suitor. *He appears genuine. How much do we know about him?*

Little to none, Ahbi sent. *Though the child here seems to like him despite my warnings to the contrary.*

If steam could have emerged from my ears, I'm certain the pilots would have been forced to release it immediately.

Sass looked up at me, eyes half-lidded as his whiskers twitched. *I see,* he sent.

Do you? I snapped my fingers at his nose to which he swatted me. *There's nothing wrong with making friends,* I sent. *Besides, he seems kind and rather humble for a demon.*

Warning signs if ever there were any, Ahbi sent.

Sassafras sighed deeply, curling up in my lap and resting his head on the back of my hand. *I fear your grandmother is right,* he sent. *Though there have been exceptions.*

I'm holding one right now. I stroked his fur with my free hand.

Touché, Ahbi sent. *Though humble will never fit our young friend here.*

Sassafras snorted and shifted into a more comfortable position, closing his eyes as we passed over the border of Ostrogotho and into the wasteland beyond, even as I wondered where my grandmother learned French.

Humble is for losers, he sent.

Anyway, I sent, *as both of you have made me very aware, the fate of Demonicon is much more important right now. And this mate ruse is for Henemordonin's benefit. I don't plan to choose for many years yet.*

You have time, Sass sent.

You don't, Ahbi shot back. *The more I see of this mess, the more I realize the only way you can save your rule is to kick his old ass from Second Seat. And the only way to do that—aside from killing him, which you seem to refuse to consider—is to marry.*

I'll deal with my grandfather, I sent with far more confidence than I dared. *And Rameranselot. When I find him. If I don't kill him, instead.*

My gaze drifted out the window, to the frothing pink falls I remembered from another trip, our first, when

Ahbi was alive and Ruler and Syd and I strangers to Demonicon. Though I had other memories of being here, they were distorted by rage and nectar fire, paired with the need to kill my sister. I preferred the innocent memories.

Dark shapes flashed through the foam, a flight of drach rising from the depths of the gorge up the flow of pink water, a formation of perfection as their wings spread wide, arrow heads pointed at the suns above. I leaned closer to the shielding with a real smile, wondering where they were off to and who was in this particular group. It had been some time since I'd seen Max, Syd's drach friend and the leader of the dragon-like creatures who were the first race.

Gasps from behind me and a grunt of irritation from Henemordonin were preceded by the heavy and powerful touch of a mind on mine as the wing of drach leveled off and came to match speed with my transport.

Ruler. Max's mind was unmistakable. I pressed my free hand to the shield as he settled close enough I could see his diamond eye clearly, a rainbow of light passing over it.

Hi, Max. Something about the drach made me giddy every time I saw them, a throwback, I could only guess, to being a little girl who dreamed of becoming a princess someday.

Might we have a word? He dipped his head toward the

ground.

Of course. I spun immediately, smile dropping away as I realized the tactical advantage I had over the rest of the demons in the transport. Even Tanasharia looked fearful of the mass of drach hovering so close, now spread out and back down the line of our entourage. "Pilots," I used my very best Ruler voice, drawing on my memories of Ahbi on her throne while she chuckled, "land."

I returned to forward facing without waiting for a reply, catching my grandfather's eyes as I did. He looked as though he wished to argue, but I glared, pointing at Max who remained level with us. "You would deny his request to speak?"

He finally shook his head and looked away. Even Henemordonin knew better than to argue with the drach.

There had been a time demons considered the drach simple animals or, at best, intelligent creatures, but beneath them. Syd's connection to the maji and Fate revealed the truth about the giant dragons. I, for one, was grateful they were on our side.

The pilots acted immediately thereafter, the transport descending rather rapidly at first. I interceded, the power of Demonicon steadying and finally taking control from them. I allowed the transport to settle to the pale yellow sand, dropping the shielding the moment the hull touched down, ignoring the other carriers as they, too, came to ground and waited.

Max landed next to me, his transformation from huge dragon to massive man happening so quickly and fluidly I barely had time to stand before he was beside me, offering his hand in aid to exit. I went with him, now grateful I'd changed clothes, stepping over the hull and onto the soft, powdered surface. Sassafras hopped over after me and the three of us left the transports behind while the sounds of anxious whispering reached me from the demons watching.

Let them watch, Ahbi sent with great satisfaction in her mental voice. *And let them be in awe. Fear is the best motivator, Meira. Never forget it.*

Oh, hush, Ahbi, Sass sent, power crackling between us.

Max's lips lifted in a barely there smile, eyes crinkling around his chrome gaze, so I knew he heard them bicker.

"Lord of the drach," I said loud enough to carry back to the others. "We are honored."

"Ruler." His deep voice boomed as his wing landed around us, remaining in dragon form, towering over us in a half-circle. I heard footsteps, knew from the pressure of power approaching my grandfather thought he should have a say in this conversation and clenched my teeth against my annoyance. Max's head tilted slightly before he went on. "It is we who are honored. Long have we meant to journey to the Seat for an official meeting. But our tasks are many and we are few."

I bowed my head to him as Henemordonin came to a

halt next to me. "Drach," he said at his most insulting. I wasn't sure what his plan might be or why he chose such an insult, but I fully expected Max to open up with a blast of fire and char my grandfather where he stood.

Instead, even better—though I really, really would have loved to have seen Henemordonin turn to a charcoal stick while Max roared the rest of the demons into wetting themselves—the drach leader ignored him. Not a twitch or a moment of recognition, nor a flicker of gaze did he offer Henemordonin. Instead, Max looked down and nodded to Sassafras.

"Lord cat," he said, the suns shining from the pale gray of his bald head, huge hand gesturing in greeting.

"Max," Sass said. "Syd says hello."

"I miss her presence," the drach said before returning his attention to me.

"What, pray tell," Henemordonin wasn't about to give up the opportunity to dominate the conversation, "is your reasoning for interrupting our journey?" He sounded more contemptuous and arrogant than angry.

Again, Max ignored him, long, dark gray robe swinging, raising soft puffs of dust from the fine sandy ground. "We felt you enter this territory and thought to take the opportunity to share a leg of your passage. With your permission, Ruler."

I opened my mouth to answer and was rudely interrupted.

"This is an official tour," Henemordonin said in a chill tone.

He did not *just say that to Max*, Sass hissed in my head.

Oh, but he did, Ahbi sent, full of horrible glee. *He really, really, did.*

This time, Max finally reacted, though again, no barbeque.

Pity, Ahbi sent.

The giant drach's head swiveled slowly to the left, his diamond gaze fixing on Henemordonin. I was tall in my platform boots, but not as tall as my grandfather. But even he was dwarfed by the massive drach leader who didn't move, or speak. He simply stared.

His assembled people began to hum, their dragon throats vibrating with sound. Nothing threatening or overpowering, but with a thread of harmony so pure and beautiful I caught my breath and held it.

I have no idea what passed between my grandfather and the massive drach leader, though I wish I could have uncovered Max's secret. For, within moments, Henemordonin's eyes dropped and he bowed his head.

He is most troublesome, Max sent while the drach continued their song, softer but still present. *Would you like me to take care of him for you?*

I laughed out loud, not even trying to hide it. Henemordonin's head turned toward me in a flash of movement, his eyes searching my face, brows pulled together. I shrugged before shaking my head.

He's my problem, I guess, I sent. *But thank you.* I could feel the fear coming from the watching demons wash toward me in waves and grinned at Max. *This whole show has succeeded where I've failed so far. You've made them fear you with minimal effort. I need to take lessons.*

Max didn't smile, but his mind felt approving. *Perhaps an escort to your destination would be appropriate*, he sent.

I think that might be an excellent idea. I beamed up at him before bowing my head. "Lord Drach," I said. "Your offer of escort is a great honor to the Seat and all demons. We accept with deepest thanks."

I didn't wait for my grandfather, not wanting to shatter the hold Max and his people had so carefully created over the watching demons. Instead, I spun and strode back to my transport, settling calmly into my chair a moment before Sassafras leaped back into my lap. Henemordonin was several steps behind me, huffing a little as he did. I liked the idea of him being the unsettled one for a change.

Rather than wait for the pilots, I took control again, powering the shielding and lifting off. It felt good to be flexing my magical muscles and, with the drach in formation around us, the remainder of our flight to Milanseme was much more relaxed. I did take the opportunity to talk to Max, however, as I wondered if he could be of help.

the planeless

When I explained the real reason for the tour, Max's mind rippled with power before settling again.

Part of the reason we have sought you out, he sent, his sparkling eye glistening as he banked to the right, following my lead. *We have been troubled, of late. There have been subtle shifts in the power holding Demonicon together and I hoped you might have information.*

That's news to me, I sent, tensing in my seat, the transport shuddering enough to make the young demons behind me meep in worry. I didn't bother to reassure them, focused on flying and on Max.

We have been gone from Demonicon for some time now, Max sent, *patrolling the veil. But upon our return only a day ago, I felt the shift in the power of the Node. I was, in fact, on my way to Ostrogotho to consult with you and your sister over the matter. But, it appears you have troubles of your own.*

Could they be connected in some way? Sassafras's quick mind was just a heartbeat ahead of mine.

I fear it is possible, Max sent. *We know how sensitive the Node is to shifts in power. If someone is stealing—or suppressing—the magic of demons, it will have an effect.*

That doesn't make sense, I sent.

It does when you consider the Node is tied to every soul on Demonicon, Max sent.

It's what? I reached for Ahbi but she was already sighing.

I thought I told you that. I'd never heard her sound

contrite. Until now.

No, Grandmother, I held my temper by a hair's breadth, *you most definitely did not*.

Irrelevant now, she sent, hurrying past the point. *Max, can something like this destabilize the Node?* She sounded worried, now.

I do not know, he sent, troubled himself. *The Node was created to support all life and all lives on the combined plane. Mass exodus of power could have a detrimental shift if it happens too quickly.*

Are you telling me if too much power is lost from too many demons, the whole thing could fall apart? My hands tightened around Sassafras who thrashed his tail several times.

Why do you think war was abolished, child? Ahbi sighed. *The idea was to keep all power here, in the combined planes, present and accessible by the Node at all times. While war and mass shifting of power could possibly unbalance the Node, this loss of power…* she mentally shook her head. *I just don't know.*

Nor do I, Max sent. *Though what would the purpose be, I wonder, to shutting demons off from their magic rather than stealing it outright?*

Because someone wants control of the Node, Sass sent quietly but with great intensity. *And know a direct assault will fail.*

All of a sudden the Planeless weren't just some cult spreading joy and peace while controlling my subjects. There was a real possibility they were bent on destroying Demonicon.

chapter twenty one

Though I wished it were otherwise, as I began my descent into Milanseme, I felt Max's regretful farewell. The drach remained hovering above us, one of their massive number sinking to the ground beside my vehicle to the shock of the gathered demons who had come to observe our arrival.

We are, unfortunately, tasked with other necessary jobs, Max sent. I looked up into the dust the landing drach raised, waving at the waiting dragons hanging in the air above. *The momentary gateway to the other Universe might have been healed, but Sydlynn's son, Gabriel's, power created cracks and lesions in our veil that require attention.*

I didn't know that, I sent.

Nor does she, he sent. *And I would prefer it remained so. I have faith the one Syd named Mabel can help you and be our go-between for the duration.* I glance to my right, realizing then the huge drach had shifted into a tall, broad-shouldered female. She bowed her head to me, diamond eyes catching the light of the suns.

Thank you, I sent, returning my focus to Max. "Drach leader," I said out loud, voice boosted by power as the entire watching body of demons fell into total silence. "It was an honor to fly with you."

"Ruler," he said in his dragon's voice, booming over the landscape without the need for magic to make himself heard, "the friendship of the drach is yours now and for all days." With that, he spun, his people following him in perfect formation. I held my ground with a thin shield to protect me, though most of my entourage squealed their protest as the sweeping wing strokes sent billows of dust and sand over everything, driving back the waiting group of demons from the city. I remained watching until the veil tore open, a gaping hole in the sky, through which the drach passed through before it sealed shut again with an almost sonic boom.

I turned, Ahbi whispering in my head, to sweep Sassafras into my arms and proceed at a calm and level pace to the border of the city. I could have taken my transport inside the city right away, but this whole show with Max and his people was far more interesting. Mabel kept step with me, at my side, none of this one step behind business to which I grinned. Having her with me was honestly a relief. I'd take all the backup I could get at this point.

"Where is Ipshinatithis?" I hoped I sounded bored and not angry.

Perfect, Ahbi laughed.

A bone-thin and most unsightly demon, his sagging skin hanging from his sharply pointed cheeks lumbered forward. His mostly bald head shone with perspiration as he bowed quickly to me, a sighing slither of a whisper emerging from his wasted lips as he forced himself up again.

"Great Ruler," he said in a voice I'm sure was meant to carry weight and polish, but came across as drily arrogant, "as your governor, I welcome you to Milanseme."

I turned my back on him, gesturing with imperial poise at my grandfather. "We shall proceed," I said as I returned to my transport. I don't think Henemordonin's face could have been more flaming crimson, his eyes burning with fury. I'd finally given him an order, for once.

Completely worth it, in every aspect.

Mabel climbed on board my vessel, glaring in silent stoicism at Tanasharia and her crew. It only took them seconds to scramble out of her gigantic way, crowding toward the back with fear in their eyes as the drach female settled on the bench behind me, taking up a surprising amount of space. Though she would never be called feminine, per se, she was a more curvy version of

Max's bulky body shape. Sleek, black hair clubbed off at the base of her neck in a tight ponytail secured with a silver clip. The rest of her was unremarkable, gray robe and pale gray skin, though, in herself, she was incredible to look at.

I turned back, certain having her with me would curtail the majority of the abuse I'd been ignoring and fighting against when it came to my cousin and the younger members of her family pack, not to mention my grandfather's penchant for yelling at me. I grinned as I pictured Mabel transforming into her drach shape and devouring him in one gulp.

I'm sorry, she sent, her mind as massive as Max's. I felt the vastness of her though she showed me only a sliver. *I don't eat people.*

Just a suggestion, I sent. *We'll work out the details later.*

The city passed beneath us, spiked spires climbing into the air around us as we descended toward the ground. I followed the slim transport guiding us in, settling on the platform of the largest building in the center of the metropolis, the top of the building peeling backward in spiny fingers to allow us to land. The moment the hull touched down, I released the shields and stepped free, ready to begin my investigation.

Four hours later I was fully prepared to drive the point of my dinner knife up the flaring nostrils of my host and dig around in what tiny brain he obviously possessed.

Temper, Ruler, Ahbi chuckled. *You'd think you were a Hayle or something with those anger issues of yours.*

I'm allowed to dream, am I not? I had to unclench my fingers from around the handle of my knife, my body's need to act taking over my good sense.

Oh, for the sake of the elements, Sassafras's voice cut in, *the two of you are absolutely insufferable. Meira, I expected more of you. And Ahbi.* The chill in his tone, his absolute disgust at our behavior, almost cracked my thin veneer, a giggle barely contained behind it. *I had thought my days of saying this to a Hayle were over, at least for a time. Ladies—pay attention!*

To what? I sat back further in the padded "throne" Ipshinatithis supplied me with. Never mind his was slightly larger. I almost made a scene, except seeing Henemordonin perched in one even smaller than mine made my night. This empty-headed buffoon wouldn't be holding his position much longer. I watched with horror and revulsion, my appetite entirely deserting me, as our host's slim fingers stogged strings of wriggling worm-like morsels into his mouth. I mean, really.

Ahbi grunted. *I've overlooked this for too long,* she sent. And sighed. *I did,* she sent, then. *Time for you to clean up my mess.*

When this is over, I sent, hugging her gently. *I know it's hard for you to remember you're dead, sometimes.*

I can't believe you two are having this conversation, Sass sent, chilly with judgment.

Oh, hush, you bossy furball, Ahbi sent, though kindly. *We're doing our best to endure.*

And, meanwhile, missing out on important conversation, he snapped.

We had? I pushed my plate away, brow furrowing as I realized Ipshinatithis spoke through the tendrils of curling creatures burrowing their ends into his goatee in an attempt to escape. My gorge rose, hands tightening on the arm rests of my seat as he chewed and talked.

"—find our fair city is loyal and prosperous," he said. A thin bit of wormy broke loose, landing heavily on the table cloth before wriggling away at a rapid pace. His quick fingers caught it with dexterity, stuffing it between his shining lips as he went on. "I realize productivity is slightly down," he smiled, bits of half-masticated and still-moving food in his teeth, "but we are doing our best to curtail the use of the new nectar in order to return to our normal schedule."

Milanseme was the main production site of the black stone from which most of Ostrogotho's city was built. The original rock came from shaping the Seat itself, carving out one half of the mountain. But such demolition ended long ago and any new building or repairs had to be done with fresh stone quarried in Milanseme's territory.

The nectar, Sassafras hissed. *Remember? This is the third time since we've sat down he's mentioned it. Things are clearly much more dire than he wants you to know. Your silence on the matter must be making him nervous.* Sass's next words came with grudging agreement. *So maybe ignoring him was a good idea. But on purpose!* Again with the whip crack of disappointment. *Not because the pair of you are acting like children.*

And how do you know we weren't paying attention? Ahbi's sly humor butted up against my demon cat's irritation.

He snarled in my head before cutting himself off completely. I watched him leap down from his place of honor at my side and stalk off to sulk.

He's right, you know. I focused more closely on Ipshinatithis though I wished it could be otherwise. At least he was done with his living dinner and had sat back to gulp large amounts of *vrena*.

"So you've said." I responded to his attempt to divert me from what was obviously an issue. "And yet, production isn't just down slightly, Governor." I didn't know that, of course I didn't. But from the look on his now sweating face, I knew I'd hit the mark as closely as I could have.

"The mine itself is having difficulties," Ipshinatithis spluttered out some of the shining red liquid, lips slick with it as he leaned toward me. "Paired with this new nectar making my workers lazy..."

Of course he would blame the workers, Ahbi snorted. *Pin*

him to the ground.

"I expect better from my leaders," I said, turning my face from him, no longer meeting his eyes in a very clear display of dissatisfaction. Henemordonin watched me, his amber eyes burning in my peripheral vision. "If you can no longer do the job I've assigned you, I will find one who can."

The fact it was your grandfather who assigned Ipshinatithis, Ahbi laughed, *back when we were still married, I do believe your little speech just killed two birds with one very well place stone.*

Now you two celebrate, Sassafras snarled. *Children.*

Ipshinatithis grunted as though I'd struck him in his non-existent belly, though I knew he wasn't looking at me.

"Forgive me, Ruler," he said.

"I think a tour is in order," I said, standing from my place at the head of the table.

Ipshinatithis scrambled to join me, eyes huge and fearful. I supposed he wasn't expecting me to want to see things for myself.

How little he knows of us, Ahbi sent.

"I will arrange it." The governor bowed, greasy, shining head as offensive as the rest of him. "Tomorrow?" I'd never heard so much hope in one word.

"Now," I said.

chapter twenty two

If the rest of the demons in attendance were upset I disrupted dinner, they made no show of it. In fact, their eagerness—that of my own court mixed with the small and slightly nervous one Ipshinatithis kept around him— told me they were looking forward to seeing what it was he wished to hide from me.

The elevator took the first large group of us, Mabel at my right side, Sequoia on my left with Sassafras in my arms again despite his continuing snit, down to street level and three further stories below before switching directions and heading for the mine located at the far edge of the city.

"The mine is a dirty and dangerous place," Ipshinatithis said, face twisted in hopeful fearfulness. "Surely my Ruler would prefer to observe from the surface where I can provide holographic surveillance."

"Your Ruler," I said, "isn't afraid of a little dirt." I met his eyes. "Or danger. I'm perfectly capable of protecting myself."

Ipshinatithis flinched back, hands clenched before him. "Of course," he whispered.

I felt my grandfather glaring and met his eyes next. He didn't say anything, finally looking away on his own and I accepted his retreat as victory.

It was several minutes on the large but cramped lift before the platform dropped another dozen or so stories before emerging into a vast, high-ceilinged space. It came to a halt at a set of stairs carved into the shining black rock so familiar to me in Ostrogotho. This stone was slightly different, though, more veined than the sparkle-filled rock of my home. Different planes, different geography.

A young-looking, earnest-faced demon rushed toward us. His thick coverall was smudged with black dust, the pores of his face dark with the same. I was so used to demons who fought for their place, it was odd to feel his focus and understand I knew far less about my people than I thought I did.

"Lord Ipshinatithis," he said, bowing to the governor. I scowled at the demon beside me who quivered slightly. He was barely 26th Plane and didn't qualify for such a title, though it was obvious to me he'd taken such liberties with his workers.

"Questorin," Ipshinatithis said. "Bow before your Ruler."

The young male fell to his knees, eyes so huge I feared they would pop from his skull as he realized who I was. "My Ruler," he whispered as he collapsed on his face to the stone, the small group of demons who had gathered behind him to watch doing the same.

I left the platform, going to his side. "Rise, Questorin," I said. "Your rank and position."

"A mere 34th Plane," he said as he stood, head still bowed. "I am a supervisor in the quarry."

I looked around, frowning. "Is this where stone is harvested?"

He glanced up, clear amber eyes startled. "No, my Ruler," he said before turning to point at a narrow tunnel leading to darkness. "The main quarry is that way."

"You will escort me." Again, I was grateful for the change in clothes I'd insisted on this morning, in equal parts my resistance of Pagomaris's need to have me doll up for dinner. Instead, my platform boots provided me moderate comfort, the black bodysuit making it easy to move around though I worried the lace draping I wore might catch on stone as I went. But I had to see for myself.

As do I, Ahbi sent.

Questorin's still startled gaze settled on Ipshinatithis, but I snapped my fingers in his face, drawing his attention again.

"Now," I said.

The court tried to follow us to the best of their ability, but, unlike me and my grandfather, the remainder of the demon court had chosen appearance over maneuverability in their clothing and within moments, we'd left them behind. I carefully stepped across a crack in the ground, Mabel drifting silently beside me despite her bulk, and began to wonder if this really was necessary.

Keep going. Sassafras perched in my arms, ears twitching as he looked ahead into the dark tunnel. *There's light at the end.*

Ipshinatithis puffed behind me, but I chose to ignore him and Henemordonin, focusing on Questorin as we went.

"Tell me of working conditions here," I said.

"They are excellent," he said, gushing a little, before pausing. "They were," he said. "The stone itself seems to be fighting us these days, my Ruler."

The light became brighter, calling us on, though not as brilliant as daylight. When we emerged from the other end and I looked out over the pit of emptiness below, I gasped. It took a great deal to shock me these days, but this did.

Tiers of worked stone with countless black holes carved in them—exits and entries, I could only guess— rose above and fell below me, like the gullet of a giant creature ready to devour us. Pinpoints of light traveled around the rings carved in the rock. The light that drew me emanated from a small hole high above, a hole, I realized, the surface of the mine.

"We're reaching the bottom, I believe," Questorin said. "The stone we bring forth seems fine, but shatters when we try to work with it. And magic that once easily carved rock from the face now creates flaws and dangerous stone chips. We've lost several workers in the past few days alone to injury."

"Another mine, perhaps?" I knew so very little about this process. I looked down, hearing the sounds of blasting rise from below as Ipshinatithis puffed his way forward and interrupted.

"Of course," he said. "There are six like this, all producing fine stone. Isn't that right, Questorin?"

The young demon met my eyes, shaking his head. "I have spoken to my fellow supervisors," he said. "They all experience the same odd problems. My Ruler, unless the source of the issue can be discovered, it's possible stone production from Milanseme will come to a complete halt."

"It will not." Ipshinatithis struck the young demon with one fist, power behind the blow, sending him spinning toward the edge. My power reached out before I thought, catching Questorin and cradling him as I drew him back to safety.

And turned to glare at Ipshinatithis.

"Things will improve." He quivered, vast belly shaking, hands wringing, face ashen. "A minor setback."

I stared with flat dislike. "They will," I said. "Once you are replaced." His protest died as I spoke further. "You think striking your subordinates for speaking the truth will solve the issue?" Anger crackled inside me. I'd been the underdog and hated to think someone like this useless sack of drach excrement had any kind of power over someone like Questorin who obviously cared about his workers. "Such failure is weakness. And I can only imagine what kind of treatment you would offer the workers of Milanseme to attempt to improve their production as it continues to fall. The failure of a process, Ipshinatithis, begins with the failure of their leadership. And that includes mine." I looked out once again over the dying mine, feeling every eye on me and knowing what I said next would cause a firestorm, but no longer willing to allow such a horrible demon power. "I will have my people review your statistics and, upon completion, if I am dissatisfied with what they find, you will be replaced." I leaned closer, his distinctive odor a mix of rotting food and sweat. "I can assure you, I will be dissatisfied."

I turned to Questorin who stared with what looked like joy. A small crowd of workers observed, smiles and nods and thanks coming my way in waves of welcoming magic. I hated to know I was right. But I could do everything now to make sure the wrong was righted.

"For now, I assign you, Questorin, to coordinate with all the mines and deliver a report to me within the day." He bowed to me, quivering though with excitement from the look on his face. "Any suggestions you might have as to the improvement and repair of the process are welcome and shall be considered."

"Thank you, my Ruler," he said. "I shall begin at once."

I brushed past my grandfather and headed back the way we came, passing by a few brave demons in fancy dress who made it this far, though too late for the show. By the time I reached the platform, I was ready to return to the surface, a faint feeling of claustrophobia holding my chest in a tight grip as I wondered if the problems in the mine were connected to the Planeless.

chapter twenty three

The walk back to my quarters was quiet, Sassafras trotting along at my feet. I expected my grandfather to appear and try to bully me, but he remained absent, much to my happiness. Not that I was left alone, though. When I entered my appointed suite, I immediately went to Bakari who waited for me by the large, square window looking out over the city.

"They are here," he said without preamble.

His pronouncement brought me to a halt as I tried to fathom what he was talking about. My mind lingered, still in the mine, worrying about—

"The Planeless." I spoke the name in a gasp of escaping air. "How many?"

He shrugged, the graceful act of an irritated animal. "Not many," he said. "Yet. They remain thin and scattered in number. But the incidents of this new nectar use are climbing and, I fear, are connected as you thought to the rise of the cult."

Why was I not surprised he knew of the nectar and my suspicions of its use? For all I knew, his sect had spies everywhere. "We need to move on this now." Sassafras leaped to a chair with a soft grunt before settling with his full tail wrapped around his paws.

"I don't see how." Sequoia sighed, sinking next to him, hand in his fur. Her gaze was full of worry. "Unless we can find a way to counteract the nectar and this odd charisma Jabuticabron claims the leader possesses, we are still in as precarious a position as we were in Ostrogotho."

The door to my quarters slammed open, Henemordonin stomping his way inside.

"Meira!" He wore his anger like a cloak while Ahbi hissed her irritation. "I would speak with you!"

Mabel moved before any of us, even Bakari, as my grandfather's power lashed out toward me. His blatant attack died against her chest, spluttering and going out as though doused in a fall of ice water. Her massive body half-transformed from broad-shouldered woman of substantial height to a half-drach combination, reminding me of the werewolves at home and how Charlotte, the princess of the werenation, and her people never fully changed into wolves, but held their human shape with animal qualities.

Mabel's face elongated in a rush of gray skin, diamond eyes glittering with drach magic as her hands clawed and tiny wings sprung from between her shoulder blades, tearing through the robe she wore as though she forgot it draped her body. A column of bright fire roared from her sharp-toothed mouth, impacting Henemordonin's shielding so hard he staggered back from her with absolute terror on his face.

The stream of fire died as fast as she produced it, Mabel placing her giant body, now part dragon, between me and my grandfather. I could no longer see her face, but the sound of her voice chilled me to the core of my bones.

"You will ask Ruler for forgiveness," she said, gravel and ice crushed under the fist of a furious drach. "And you will beg her not to allow me to devour you."

I thought you didn't eat people. I could barely contain my surprise or the joy I felt knowing I had Mabel at my side. While I loved my other friends and advisors, the pure fear now masked behind hurt and arrogance on my grandfather's face made me want to kiss the drach woman.

I will make an exception, she sent. *This once.*

With slow, steady steps I joined her, facing off with my grandfather while he glared at me.

And waited.

And waited.

He cracked long before I did, smoke drifting from between Mabel's lips, a rumbling growl reminding him of her intent.

"Call off your dog," he snapped.

"You can yell at me all you want," I said, amusement gone cold and angry. "But to the drach, you owe respect, Henemordonin. The first race has earned it."

"She threatened me." So much indignation in those words, I could barely stand him.

"She defended the Ruler of Demonicon," I said. "Something Mabel chose of her own free will. I am honored beyond words she sees fit to do so." I bowed my head to her and she returned the gesture, still smoking. "We seem to have a disagreement with who exactly rules our planes. A small discrepancy you've exploited over the years. I thought I made it clear to you," I turned my back on him, "I would no longer tolerate such behavior from my Second Seat. But you've made it obvious you have no intention of showing me the respect of my position. And so, if Mabel choses to eat you, I won't stand in her way."

Henemordonin spluttered while I turned back, the drach female advancing ever so slightly on him. "Or," I said, "you can participate in this conversation like a civilized demon and actually help for once instead of doing everything you possibly can to hinder me."

To my grandfather's credit, he squared his shoulders and nodded. "I still wish to speak to you," he said, soft growl now barely audible in his voice.

"And it's time you were filled in on what's happening on Demonicon," I said. I strode to the window, only then realizing Bakari was gone. How he'd vanished I had no idea, though I understood. If my grandfather realized the demon was talking to me behind his back, Henemordonin would no longer trust him—if he did now.

"There is a new strain of nectar on the streets," I said. "Ipshinatithis already mentioned it."

"I am aware," Henemordonin said. Mabel backed off, returning to more-or-less human form though her eyes never left my grandfather.

Maybe it should have irritated me to know he was already in possession of the knowledge, but I shrugged instead. "We believe this nectar is a forerunner for a more dangerous assault on our people." I leaned against the window frame, arms crossed over my chest. "A cult rising in power calling themselves the Planeless."

Henemordonin grunted. "Impossible," he said. "The Planeless are harmless. They preach peace and unity."

This time I was angry. "You knew about them."

"Of course," he snapped. Mabel's soft growl pulled him back from shouting. I was going to love having her around. "It is your failing as Ruler you've only just discovered them."

He did not just say that to you, Ahbi snarled.

"Considering you've done everything you possibly

can to keep me tied down, powerless and out of touch," I shot back, fingers digging into the crystals embedded in my lace robe, "the fact I uncovered this information at all is a miracle."

He didn't comment, though his glare intensified.

"Tell me what you know." I matched his glare, the understanding of his uselessness returning. Even more now I saw the frustrated and power hungry boy inside him, sullen and bitter over being cast aside by Ahbi, doing everything in his power to pay me back for what she'd done.

I'm sorry, child, Ahbi sighed in my head. *He wasn't always so pathetic.*

I don't want to hear it, I snapped as she flashed me a memory of a tall, handsome, self-possessed demon with a ready smile and a passion for life she admired. *He's not that person anymore.*

He isn't, she sent. *And I wonder if he ever really was.*

"Tell me, Second Seat," I said, "what you have planned to stop them?"

"Nothing." Henemordonin crossed his own arms, glare gone to flat blankness.

He has to be kidding. Ahbi spluttered. *You damned fool.*

"I agree with their philosophy," Henemordonin said at his pompous best. "And so did your father."

"Dad was involved in this?" I couldn't bring myself to believe my father would willingly participate in something so frightfully stupid.

"Not directly," Henemordonin said. "But his demonocracy laid the foundation for their beliefs. Think about it, Meira." I should have snapped power at him for using my name but my horror at his sudden fanaticism made me want to throw up. "Demons at peace with each other. The progress we could make! So much time and power wasted on petty arguments, small-minded bickering, and the laws keeping us from evolving into our true and natural way of being."

"Empty of power and enslaved to a cult leader who feels like sorcery," I said.

Henemordonin flinched but his enthusiasm remained, if hyper-focused on me, a pointed blade with power and persuasion pushing it through my shielding. "It's time to shed your grandmother's false and old-fashioned influence," he said, wheedling and soft, almost kind despite the shiver of revulsion his attention created in me. "She is holding you—and all of Demonicon—back from our path to perfection."

I didn't need Ahbi's constant swearing in my head to trigger my own anger.

"Ahbi Sanghamitra led our people for longer than most demons are alive," I said. "She kept them safe and prosperous for all that time. You dare question her and her motives? Or her loyalty to demonkind?"

"I question her ability to see the truth," he said,

dropping his false attempt at connecting on an emotional level. "And, through her influence, I question you. Always."

"The feeling is mutual." I hit him hard with power, sending him back another step while Mabel tensed further, ready to act on my command. "The next time I find out you're holding out on me, I'm going to feed you to Mabel."

Henemordonin's scowl deepened the lines on his once handsome face, craters of unhappiness pulling down the thick brow over his eyes, making his mouth curve into a slash of displeasure under his thick beard.

"I want all the information you have on the Planeless," I said, turning my back on him. "Mabel will accompany you and ensure you hand everything over to Sequoia." I heard her skirts rustle as Sass's sister stood immediately. I held my position until I heard the door to my quarters close and Sassafras sighed.

"He's an idiot," my demon cat said. "But a dangerous idiot."

"To himself, at this point," I said, sinking down next to him, taking over the place Sequoia had sat. "Mabel will make him a bedtime snack if he comes against me."

"Openly," Bakari said.

I jumped out of the chair with a squeak of fear, hands pressed to my chest, power rippling in a thick shield around Sass and I. The assassin smiled, teeth flashing.

"You've been here the whole time," I said.

"I have." He held out one hand, the fingers disappearing in a wavering distortion before returning again. "A simple trick, to convince the air to allow me to take its form. But useful."

"You can say that again." Sassafras swatted in Bakari's direction. "I think you're right, though. Henemordonin is much more likely, at this point, to stop his overt attacks—if veiled in the false concern of Second Seat—and find a way to pull the rug out from under you without showing his involvement."

"Not if I can prevent it." Bakari laughed this time, making me shiver. He bowed. "You have the drach to watch your front," he said, "and I have your back." And I could trust him. Sure, I could. "In the meantime, Henemordonin's sympathies concern me greatly. Especially since I was unaware of his thoughts on the Planeless. For some reason, your grandfather has kept his opinions carefully hidden from everyone." His smile was gone, little frown worse in many ways than his cold laughter. "His altered activities may be more insidious than just harming you."

I choked on that thought. "There's no way he's involved with the cult," I said. "My grandfather might agree with them in principle, but the demon is power hungry."

"Perhaps," Bakari said. "But I wouldn't put it past

him to use this crisis to his advantage, at the very least."

"That, I believe," I said. "Keep me posted."

I watched him leap out the window with my heart in my throat, partially from his daring jump and partially at the thought I might be wrong about my grandfather after all.

CHAPTER TWENTY FOUR

Bilhaeder appeared on the horizon on the other side of the lush rainforest. Rainbow domes beckoned to me while I piloted the transport through a thermal pocket and on a landing trajectory for the city's main terminal. A quick briefing with the pilots I no longer needed showed me exactly where to go. Unlike Milanseme, Bilhaeder had no access to transports and so we were forced to land in the same location as cargo vessels.

As we circled the city, our long line of transports winding out behind me in a half circle, reminding me of a colorful, child's train set magically sailing through the sky, I pondered what Questorin told me just that morning when he came to report his findings.

"Forgive me, Ruler," the mine supervisor said from his knees with his head bowed. "But things are much worse than I'd been led to believe. The mine I am in charge of has been much less affected by whatever is hampering our ability to harvest stone."

A quick rundown on the details made me sweat. Three of the six mines were now completely out of operation, two more down to a trickle of production. Only the mine I'd seen and one other maintained a level of productivity, though Questorin was the first to admit it was declining rapidly. While merely building stone, without import beyond that task, it was the main source of income for the city. Without the stone, the Seat would have to take up the slack of providing for the people.

"I have no idea why," he said, real grief and guilt in his voice. "I beg you, Ruler, don't take this out on the workers. It's not their fault."

I purposely had Ipshinatithis attend our meeting and turned to him with fury. "This mess is of your making," I said. "You may not be responsible, but choosing to keep the crisis from me has led to a paralysis of stone mining and brought manufacturing to a standstill."

"But, Ruler," he whined, groveling before me, "I did send word to Ostrogotho."

Henemordonin, Ahbi hissed.

I tasked Ipshinatithis with cleaning up the city of all sources of the new nectar and Questorin with coming up with new ways to harvest the stone without causing more problems. I wished I could have stayed, feeling as though I'd finally been able to help, at least offer some guidance, to my people. But I had other tasks ahead of me and the possible source of my troubles lay ahead.

Sassafras sat curled in my lap, his favorite position, though more to keep in close contact with me, I assumed, than for the reciprocation of comfort.

We need to be careful here, he sent as I settled the transport onto the platform. Mabel shifted behind me, her power touching mine as Sassafras went on. W*e have no idea how far the Planeless have spread.*

You want me to go back to Ostrogotho and let Henemordonin handle this? I rose, Sass lifted into my arms as I turned and swept my gaze over the empty platform. I expected some kind of greeting from my local governor, had made sure Ipshinatithis sent word ahead. But aside from a few startled transport workers, the large, flat space remained empty.

The soft breeze of the arrival of the remaining transports in the entourage gave me a gentle shove forward. I stepped over the edge of the hull and to the shining, white-blocked surface, its polished stone the direct opposite of the sharp black I was accustomed to. I'd dressed in white today on impulse and was glad of it, though Pagomaris still sulked over my lack of interest in her fantastic getups. Instead, my favorite chrome boots tromped down on the deck, a silvery white bodysuit, a match for the black one yesterday, belted tight with a thick, floor-length coat trimmed in fur as silver as Sass's.

the planeless

Confused and now slightly irritated, I stomped to the edge of the platform, surveying the city below only one story down. The entire bay was open to the air, and, as I reached a position where I could see clearly, I realized a large crowd had gathered in the massive greeting area below the arrival point. I hardly had a moment to register their watchfulness, to hear the roar of their recognition before a tall, white-haired demon in a robe as gleaming as mine strode up the stairs alone, a staff in one hand and a mysterious smile on his handsome face.

Even his horns were white, sparkling in the suns newly risen. And not painted or capped, either. I could almost see through them, so translucent were they, as were the thick fingernails on his hand clasping the staff.

He reached the last step and joined me on transport deck, smiling down at me with so much gentleness I sagged slightly from his attention.

Meira! Sassafras's mind slapped mine, jerking me free of the soft, powdery sweetness of this demon's presence. *Pay attention!*

Even Ahbi shook herself, wound up in him. *I feel no magic*, she whispered.

Neither did I. But he carried power, that much was certain, even before he opened his mouth and spoke in a voice of a saint.

"Welcome, Senne Hathenemeria," he said. "We welcome you."

Below us, the watching demons—at least a few thousand of them—swayed in answer, an almost joyful sound escaping them.

He owns Bilhaeder, Sass sent, tense with anxiety. *Or, at least, part of it.*

That much was obvious. "I expected my governor," I said, pulling every ounce of control I could from Ahbi and the power of Demonicon to keep my voice steady and cold.

They heard it, the watching beloved of this demon, and protested with their voices.

He simply shook his head, strands of white hair swaying free, good humor in his eyes. They made me shiver, those eyes, the palest amber I'd ever seen, almost as white as the rest of him. Even his skin was barely red, more pinkish, but he didn't appear sickly or hideous as I expected someone of his coloring might. Instead, as he stood there, shoulders curved toward me, kindness on his face, I compared him to an angel.

This is very, very bad, Sass sent. *Meira.*

I know, I sent. *I do. But Sass… what if he's not the problem?* It had to be the Planeless leader standing before me. His undeniable charisma almost made me swoon, though I had help enough to stand my ground against him.

Ruler, Mabel's heavy voice broke the spell this demon held over me. *While it may feel otherwise, I can assure you, there is nothing of goodness or light in this being.*

His eyes flickered from mine to the towering drach behind me and, for the briefest moment, I saw through the façade he'd built around himself, felt clearly the darkness in him wrapped in a candy-coating of falsehood. When he met my gaze again, emptiness flared inside me, eating away at my soul. I blocked it even as the monster in me—my demon's unquenchable desire for power—rose with a snarling hunger so strong I almost swayed. I'd only felt it once before, when I'd stripped one of my father's possible marriage matches of her magic after she tried to have me killed. This was the reason we demons only combated for fractions of each other's magic. Taking all woke a ravenous drive so overwhelming Syd was right when she pegged it as the monster within.

The darkness fell quiet and died away under the surge of my darkest need. No longer challenged, the starving creature inside me faded into the background once again. I had no time to ponder what the feeling meant, just grateful I was free of him. And, though I know he must have tried, I no longer felt the pressure of his special brand of control.

"People of Demonicon," he said, turning from me, voice booming out over the crowd, "you see before you the demon who rules you." He stepped away from me, soft smile still in place, oozing kindness to the point I thought I might be sick. "This is what we have become."

He swept one arm back, his staff lighting at the tip with a flare of white flame. "The good and honest souls of this plane slave for a mere pittance while the ruling class," he gestured to me, to those gathering behind me as my court came closer, "flaunt their wealth and privilege." He shook his head again, soft sparks of white falling from him like shooting stars while the demons below grumbled and darkened. But there was no anger in his voice, only chastisement as though I were a child he needed to sweetly take to task. "There is a better way," he said directly to me, though his voice continued to carry. "The way of the Planeless."

The crowd below burst into cheering, hugging each other, their anger replaced so rapidly with joyful euphoria I could only guess he controlled them all.

Indeed, Mabel sent. *Not a free will among them.*

Can you change that? If she could cut their bond to him here and now, maybe I could turn this around.

I cannot, she sent, sounding perplexed. *Whatever hold he has, it's not just through power.*

The nectar. Sassafras hissed in my head. *Deal with him.*

The demon's teeth flashed as he offered his free hand. "I am Xeoniteridone," he said. "And I welcome you to the ranks of the righteous."

"I am your Ruler," I said, drawing heavily on Ahbi for support. "And these demons are my people."

Xeoniteridone's expression saddened as the crowd

below groaned.

"You do not own them," he said. "They are free."

More euphoria. *He's going to break them if he keeps jerking them around like that*, Sass snapped.

I barely heard him. My attention was long lost as I glanced down the steps at three demons who stood waiting for their leader. Dressed in the same white robes, though their coloring remained red and black, they looked like acolytes or some kind of servants. But it wasn't their presence that bothered me so much. It was the sight of Rameranselot's handsome face that brought me to an abrupt halt.

He stared at me with blank eyes, not a hint of who he was in his expression. And when I reached for him with my magic, I touched the same empty power I'd felt all along.

Now, as though my ability to feel it had woken to full attention, I felt it everywhere, not just in Ram. The blank feeling permeated the area, the demons below, even Xeoniteridone himself. When I looked up and met his icy eyes, his smile hadn't faded.

"Please, consider our message," he said, backing away. "Peace and love for all demons. It is a worthy goal, Senne. One I hope you will come to embrace."

Xeoniteridone spun and walked back down the stairs, Ram and the other two demons joining him. I watched with horror, wishing there was something I could do, and almost slamming the retreating Xeoniteridone in the back with power.

It would kill him, I sent to the others.

Possibly, Mabel sent. *Though you have no idea what protections surround him.*

And if you fail, you will have a mass of vengeful demons ready to tear you apart. Sassafras snorted. *Let him go. Now that we know his whole love and peace thing is an act, we can move forward in blocking him.*

I don't see how, I sent, suddenly queasy. *How do I combat this?*

I gestured at the crowd of demons, parting in a sea of happy bodies, to allow Xeoniteridone to pass through. Without a backward glance, they followed him, a massive wall of red and black.

The fact Ahbi, Sass and Mabel remained silent didn't help me feel any better.

chapter twenty five

I was still trying to decide what to do, the retreating mass of the Planeless followers thinning as they left, when a small and harried group of demons rushed from a building on my right and hurried toward us.

It was hard to ignore the whisperings of my court and the clear pressure of Henemordonin's magic and force myself to watch as the group below ascended the stairs with rapid and uncoordinated steps.

The demon in the lead bowed deeply to me as he reached the top of the platform, panting and deeply red in the face, his amber eyes muddied with worry.

"My Ruler," he croaked out my title, "forgive our tardiness. I am Celuniumtrix, your representative here in Bilhaeder. I believed you to be arriving an hour from now or I would have been here myself to greet you."

"Instead," I snapped, "I was greeted by some

fanatical cult leader and his brain-wiped followers." Was it fair to take out my frustration and fear on this lowly public servant? Perhaps not, but there was no one else, and I deemed him fortunate I didn't strip his power then and there for being incompetent.

Temper, dear, Ahbi sent.

The demon paled, bobbing his head, his throat working as he swallowed so audibly my lips lifted in disgust.

"Xeon," Celuniumtrix whimpered. "My city is overrun with the Planeless."

"And yet this is the first I've heard of it," I said, tapping my chrome platform boot on the polished white stone. "You deemed this detail uninteresting and not worthy of your Ruler's attention?"

"But, my Ruler," he said, spluttering over the double "r", "I did send word to Ostrogotho, weeks ago."

I'm going to tear out his heart and eat it in front of him, Ahbi snarled.

There's nothing we can do about it here in the open, Sassafras sent. I almost wished his voice of reason wasn't quite so reasonable. *Let's retreat to privacy and talk this out before we make any hasty decisions.*

Like murdering Second Seat right here and now? I suppressed a shudder so violent I knew it would go on and on forever if I let it escape. *You're probably right.*

I gestured for Celuniumtrix to rise, his followers

doing the same, though they looked as nervous as he did.

"We would be seen to our quarters," I said, "and then I would like a full accounting of the productivity of this city and the breakdown of the hold the Planeless has over its citizens."

The governor paled, bobbing his head to me though he appeared as though he might expire from fear at any moment.

I followed him, my friends around me, ignoring Henemordonin for the moment. I left him to wrangle the waiting members of court in favor of retreat to somewhere quiet where I could decide if I wanted to cry uncontrollably or throw something.

We passed through the quiet morning and into the half-circle building from which Celuniumtrix and his people emerged into a large atrium that took up the majority of the first floor. Open balconies for each story above towered overhead. I was led to the center of the room where a platform waited and held myself quiet as the elevator launched skyward.

Within moments, I was in a private suite taking up fully half of the top of the dome, Celuniumtrix bowing his way out so quickly, his need to escape me so powerful, I let him go. There would be time to drill him for information later. For now, I had to regroup and figure out what just happened and what I was going to do to keep my plane from falling apart.

Bakari's appearance didn't surprise me so much this time as he drifted from thin air to greet me with a scowl.

"They are many in number, here," he said. "Far more than I was led to believe."

"Ram was with them," Sequoia said, distress on her tiny face as she took Sassafras from my arms. "He looked so…"

"Vacant." I spun and paced, my habit picked up from Syd. I could understand completely why she stomped her way around in circles when she was upset. There was a satisfaction to aggressive movement when no other action was possible.

"We need to rescue Ram," I said, stopping to face Bakari. "Can you extract him?"

"Risky," Sassafras said.

"But necessary," I said.

Your hormones aside, Ahbi sent, *he's the least of our troubles, child.*

My nostrils flared as I held in my temper. "We need to know if whatever has been done is reversible," I said. "And Ram is the perfect candidate to test. We know he is loyal to me, unlike some random demon we might liberate from the pack. Correct?"

Everyone nodded, including my grumbling grandmother.

"I will do my best," Bakari said and vanished.

I was already turning to Mabel. "Was it sorcery?" She

wasn't a sorcerer herself, per se, but like the maji, she had access to that particular brand of magic.

The drach female frowned. "I felt the emptiness of sorcery," she said, "but not the source. Which makes me wonder if we're dealing with something new."

"Could Theridialis's predictions about the new nectar be true?" I addressed this question to Sequoia and her brother, Sass's furry body perched in her lap. "And could the nectar be interfering with what Mabel is feeling?"

Sequoia shrugged delicately. "It's possible," she said. "Father is still working on uncovering the components. He promised he would contact us when he had any further information."

At least he was safely working at the Seat instead of exposed in his tower in Ostrogotho. I'd left Jabuticabron and a large number of my personal guard—loyal only to me—to guard him. His task was too important to risk him.

"We need more time to examine this Xeon," Sassafras said. "We had little time this morning. Clever, very clever." The demon cat's eyes flared. "I almost appreciate his strategy. Pin us down and use surprise to gain the upper hand. He obviously has someone on the inside of the government to know when we were arriving and to block the governor's knowledge. Which means some of the Planeless must remain in control of their faculties in order to carry out his wishes."

"It's likely they all do," Mabel sent. "They did not feel mindless to me, merely influenced."

And yet, there was no magic, Ahbi sent. Her worry matched mine. *We must arrange to meet and talk with this demon on our own terms.*

"Agreed," Mabel said while Sassafras and Sequoia both nodded. Nice of Ahbi to share with everyone.

A hesitant knock on the door sent Pagomaris scurrying. A slim and shaking young demon girl curtsied to me as my aide ushered her inside. The poor little thing looked terrified as she looked around at the gathered demons and giant drach hovering around me.

"My Ruler," she said in a squeaking voice, "a luncheon has been prepared in your honor. My father asks you to join us."

"You are the daughter of Celuniumtrix?" No need to scare the poor dear any more than I already had. I smiled at her, forcing down my stress.

"I am." She curtsied again, dimples perfect on her round cheeks. "I am called Unasaria, my Ruler."

"We will join you presently," I said. "If you would wait outside a moment."

Her nervousness seemed to fade as she smiled up at me again. "Thank you, my Ruler."

I waited until the girl was gone behind the closed door, Pagomaris retreating with her, before I returned my attention to my watching friends.

"Lunch," I sighed. "And then we set up court."

"And?" Sassafras wriggled free of his sister and landed softly on the carpet, sashaying his way toward me.

"And," I said, "we summon Xeoniteridone and find out what he's really up to."

One look at Celuniumtrix's nervous face as his daughter led us into the dining hall and I knew this wasn't going to be an ordinary luncheon. And any opportunity I might have to arrange things to my advantage when it came to Xeoniteridone had just gone out the very large window at the back of the room.

He sat at the head of the table, his white staff resting against the chair, robe pooled around him as he perched with thoughtful contemplation in my seat.

The governor rushed to my side, bowing and sweating, his daughter slipping out of the line of fire as Celuniumtrix fell to his knees before me.

"My Ruler," he said. "The Planeless leader is joining us for our meal."

Oh, he is, is he? Ahbi glared through my eyes at the softly smiling Xeoniteridone. He made no move to rise, gesturing at the seat next to him as though inviting me to take a lower position at his side.

I moved without thinking, striding to the far end of the table, sitting, instead, in the governor's seat. A brief burst of magic increased the chair's size to rival that of

Xeoniteridone's. I placed myself gracefully on its surface while my court hurriedly rearranged themselves to make my end of the table dominant.

Xeoniteridone smiled at me the entire time, his false calm unruffled. Only the scowl on Henemordonin's face told me my grandfather was angry at my decision, though I wondered why, considering giving up status meant giving up power.

This might not be ideal circumstances, Sassafras sent in a very tight mental connection, most likely worried, as I was, Xeoniteridone could hear our private communication if we weren't careful. *But at least we have a chance to study him. And, it appears, he is either wholly arrogant or powerful enough he doesn't have to worry, because he's come alone.*

Would I have had the courage to do so? I wasn't so sure.

It took only until the first course was served for Xeoniteridone to speak up.

"Such expensive fare," he said of the spiced soup, its scent wafting across the table. A few of my court paused in their eager slurping to listen. "While the people of Demonicon eat swill."

If he's trying to stir sympathy with this crowd, he's preaching to the wrong choir. Ahbi sat back in my mind, full of cynicism.

Why, if she was right, were some of them lowering their spoons, staring at their bowls with frowns on their faces?

the planeless

He influences them, Mabel sent. *The same influence you felt, though much more subtle.* She was correct. The emptiness hovered over us, undulating and whispering support for him as Xeoniteridone pushed his bowl away and bowed his head.

"Why waste it?" I lifted my spoon and took a healthy bite, though the flavor wasn't to my taste. As the court watched, I emptied my bowl, no one else moving or saying anything as Xeoniteridone's head slowly lifted. He watched me eat with his same smile until I patted at the corner of my mouth with my napkin and sat back. "Delicious," I said.

"Much like the souls of our people," he said. "Souls that have fed you and your family for centuries uncounted."

I *counted them*, Ahbi grumbled.

"You speak of the Node," I said. *What is he after?* Neither Sassafras nor Mabel answered while Ahbi continued to listen with me. "The power that protects and sustains all demons."

"So you say," Xeoniteridone said, sighing in exaggerated sorrow. "But what proof do the people of Demonicon have the Node exists for that reason? For all we know, we humble and lowly beings, its only purpose is to keep us angry and full of hate."

And we thought Henemordonin was a master manipulator, Ahbi sent.

Agreed, I said. *He has nothing on this demon.*

"Demonicon exists only because the Node exists," I said, Ahbi coming out in me as we spoke together. "Without the Node, we would return to the scattered planes that once made up demon existence, ruled by the need to kill and destroy. Thanks to the Node and its support, and the laws surrounding it, demons have been allowed to evolve past our base nature and create this great society we enjoy."

"Not so great," Xeoniteridone said, still sorrowful as the emptiness descended further, "for the lesser demons of Demonicon."

I felt Mabel try to push back against the blank cloud hovering, but could tell, as her power slipped through it, she had no success.

I am baffled, she sent to me, feeling slightly shaken. *I have never encountered anything like this before. I must alert the others of my race.*

Before she could rise, I sent anxiety to her. *I need your observations*, I sent. *Please, there is time after this charade is over.*

Very well, she sent, massive body relaxing beside me where she'd taken the seat Henemordonin would normally have claimed. *But this matter has just become most urgent.*

She wasn't exaggerating. As I refocused on the gathering, I saw heads nodding in agreement, not just of the governor's people but my own court, those I thought would be above such caring. They were the most selfish demons I knew. And here they were, falling under Xeoniteridone's spell.

Powerful magic, indeed.

"I can see you will not listen to reason." Xeoniteridone rose from his seat, his staff in his hand, face troubled, white glitter cascading from his skin as he gestured toward me with his free fingers. "A pity. You, Senne, could have led us in this march toward our ultimate evolution."

"Don't even consider threatening me," I said, even as I wished he would. Mabel could have traded eating my grandfather for this lying piece of crap.

Xeoniteridone's face crumpled in grief. "I would never do such a thing," he said. "Threats and anger are your domain." The cloud finally lowered over the gathering, settling directly on my people. I felt Sassafras shudder, shielding myself and those closest to me from it as quickly as I could, but wincing as the smoke-like emptiness slipped through all my protections. "I can hope, one day, you will see the light. And I will rejoice on that day, Senne. Until then, I wish you well, but more so, I wish peace, prosperity and light for our people."

I remained where I was, watching as he left, glowering as the gathered court did the same. Whatever spell he cast over them seemed to snap the moment he left, though, leaving me with shaken demons who whispered among themselves as the cloud vanished.

From the worried and anxious looks on their faces, however, I knew he'd left a far bigger impression than I would have liked.

ChAPTER TWENTY SIX

I stared into the gap in the veil, wincing at the angry look on Syd's face as she stepped through and came to a halt with her arms crossed over her chest.

"Oh. My. Swearword." Power flickered around her as her agitation grew. "This is a mess, Meems."

She has no right to be angry with us, Ahbi huffed.

I'm not, Syd sent, equally as huffy. *But it's time to act.*

Agreed, Ahbi sent, mollified.

So Mabel couldn't stop it? Syd paced, taking away my need to do the same. I held my ground as she moved quickly from one end of the room to the other. I was grateful I sent the others away before I called her, if only because speaking to her and Ahbi this way felt the most comfortable.

No, I sent. *And she was thrown by the fact. She said she would speak to Max and see if the drach could come up with anything.*

What about the maji? Ahbi's question was met with a heavy sigh from my sister.

Like the maji ever did anything that wasn't in their own best interest. She stewed a bit before catching hold of her temper. *They're useless.*

A gust of air hit me, so powerful it broke through the shielding around the window. A massive black shape appeared, morphing into Mabel as she leaped in mid-transformation, landing lightly for so huge a person, on the carpet. As calm as ever, she spun to face us, her gray robe settling around her.

It was nice to have her back after a quick disappearance after dinner to alert her people.

I have spoken with Max, she sent to all of us. *And though he understands the dangerous nature of this matter, he has uncovered further damage to the veil and cannot commit the full support of the drach nation to this incident until the hurt is healed.*

"Um, what?" Syd stopped pacing the moment Mabel arrived, and now she looked like the drach female hit her on the way in. "What damage to the veil?"

"He has kept this information from you," Mabel said, "though I have long advised him to share the details of the problem. It would appear, when your son was forced to open a way to the other Universe, he caused severe strain to be placed on our veil. I wouldn't doubt the other Universe suffers the same. Fortunately, the gateway was closed before tears between the Universes could become permanent. But we have spent the last several years doing what we can to heal the damage."

Syd's mouth hung open before snapping shut. I knew the angry look on her face, the way her hands clenched at her sides. She wasn't mad at Mabel any more than she'd been angry with me over this mess we were in.

No, my very powerful sister was right now beating the crap out of herself internally over something she couldn't have prevented if she wanted to.

"He should have told me," she said, voice deep and echoing, another sure sign she was wrapped up in guilt. There were so many times I envied Syd her power and importance, that I felt less than her. But when I saw just how hard she was on herself over every single thing that went wrong, I, instead, felt powerful empathy for her. Being Ruler was hard enough without having to worry about the literal fate of the Universe.

Mabel bowed her head to Syd. "Indeed," she said. "I will take you to him now so you might explain to him the error of his ways."

I snorted a laugh, despite everything, as Mabel's crystalline eyes settled on me. "Did you just make a joke?"

"I have an excellent sense of humor," she said in her deadpan voice.

Syd was grinning now, too, so I was grateful to Mabel

for shattering my sister's obsession with what she'd done wrong.

"Great idea." She joined the tall drach at the window before turning and grabbing me. I hugged her tightly, her power wrapping around me. Tears prickled my eyes. Syd always put everyone else first.

"We'll be back," she said, pushing me away. "With Max. And we'll figure this out." She winked at Mabel. "After I kick his drach ass."

I watched them go, Mabel taking Syd's hand and leaping out into the night. I leaned out, holding back the shield so I could watch them. The drach transformation was instant, Syd soaring like a superhero through the air before her iridescent magic flared and she landed on Mabel's back. The air above them crackled and tore, the pair diving through the veil in a display that gave me goosebumps.

It was a few seconds before I backed away from the window, wishing I could have gone with them. When I turned, I gasped a breath at the sight of Elph standing by the door, watching me.

"My Ruler," he bowed to me. "I'm sorry to intrude. But I hoped I could offer some help or counsel in this troubled time."

Part of my instant hesitation came from Ahbi. *We have no idea if we can trust him*, she sent.

He seems unaffected by Xeon. I forced myself to relax and

gestured for him to come closer. "You seem unimpressed with the Planeless leader."

Elph's brows drew together, his shoulders tightening as he shrugged. "The demon carries great persuasion with him," he said. "And I admit, when he spoke, I felt oddly drawn to his argument. But when he left us, I seemed to wake from a dream, as though a cloud had lifted from my mind." He shook his head, eyes full of concern. "Such control cannot be a natural thing, though I felt no magic from him."

I nodded. "What of the others?" My suddenly dry throat begged for a drink. I poured two glasses of *vrena* and offered him the second which he took with another bow. "What does my court say of this Xeon?"

Elph sat next to me as I sank into a thickly padded sofa, crossing my heavy platform boots.

"Worry abounds," he said, "and some are actually arguing for more information on this peace the Planeless offer." Elph sighed. "I never believed such a selfish society could ever accept the control that would come with religion."

"Me either," I said, staring down into the dark red liquid in my goblet. "And yet, here we are."

"Henemordonin addressed us all," he said, leaning closer, concern turned to worry. "He encourages us to investigate this religion further." Anger boiled in my stomach as he went on. "He gave the impression you yourself were behind the edict."

"I can assure you," I said with clenched teeth and fury, "I was not."

"I could not bring myself to believe so," Elph said, relief coming over his face. "What are we to do, my Ruler?" Before I could answer, he leaned suddenly away, head down. "Forgive me," he said. "I overstep my bounds. You have not taken me into your confidence, and I could only dream such a thing could be possible."

He can't be this nice and not have an agenda, Ahbi sent.

Grandmother, I sent. *Shut up.*

Elph's face lifted, eyes sparkling with earnestness. "I am here for you, my Ruler," he said, "in whatever capacity you require of me. I will stand at your side and defend you from all comers until you tell me to go. And even then, I will protect and worship you from a distance."

Heady stuff, Ahbi sent. *Don't let it go to your ego, child.*

I thought, I growled to her, *I told you to shut up.*

"Elph," I said out loud, "here's the skinny." And over the next fifteen minutes or so, I proceeded to fill him in on everything we learned. I even found myself dropping some of my more formal language, my comfort level with him rising as he listened intently, nodding and making agreeing sounds until I wound down and sank back again, taking a long drink to soothe my tired throat.

"Though I know nothing of sorcery," he said, "I do

know Bilhaeder." I looked up, caught the excitement in his face. "I spent years here, you recall. And, because of that knowledge, I'm thinking it would be simplicity itself to track down Xeoniteridone and his people and observe them without their knowledge."

I don't know about this, Ahbi sent.

I do. I cut her off as I contemplated the idea. "It would be good to see Xeoniteridone in action," I said, "without him knowing I was there."

"Exactly." Elph set his goblet aside. "As long as we go quickly and under the protection of darkness, I'm certain we can uncover what he's really up to."

"Now, you mean." I stood, nodding. "I'll have to change." My white outfit would stand out. I shed the heavy coat, a touch of magic transforming the white body suit into black. "Some robes, perhaps." The idea of escaping these quarters, of actually doing something, fired my blood and the demon inside me. Even Ahbi seemed to relent and join in my enthusiasm.

"I have just the thing," Elph said as the door opened and Sequoia entered, Sassafras at her feet.

"You'd better have four of those things," my demon cat said. "We're coming with you."

Eavesdropping, cat? Ahbi's laughter made me frown.

Naturally, he sent, staring up at me with irritation on his pushed-in cat face. "You really thought we'd let you go alone?"

"Well, you can't go like that," I said.

"I realize as much." His heavy tail thrashed. "A little magic, my Ruler, if you please."

Elph left with Sequoia as I focused on Sassafras. "Hold still."

A gust of air by the window and Mabel returned. I waved to her as the power of Demonicon wrapped around the demon cat and pushed. He expanded much as she had shrunk on her way inside, though his transformation wasn't real. When Sass's power had been stripped from his demon body and placed into the body of the cat he inhabited, Theridialis had kept the form just in case Sass returned one day. But the body didn't survive, the cellular degradation too much for him to reclaim when he had the chance. And so, the only way he could survive was in the cat's furry form.

Transforming him this way would only last a few hours at best, but would be long enough for us to do our investigation. I smiled into his eyes, the eyes I remembered from his short time as a human teenager, savoring the sight of him as human before adding demon elements. Horns sprouted from his temples, winding back from his face as his eyes turned from dark brown to deep amber. He grinned at me, winked, though I could see the old hurt behind his eyes and wished there was a way to make this permanent.

No you don't, he sent. *You'd miss me as a cat.*

Silly, I sent, hugging him, *I love you no matter what.*

Elph and Sequoia returned at that very moment. Sass's sister rushed to him with a soft cry, hugging him as I did. I let them have a moment, taking a heavy black robe from Elph's hands.

"Scholar's robes," he said with an embarrassed smile. "We'll return them before they know they are gone. But they will serve our purpose and should disguise us well enough."

I slipped into the heavy black fabric, edged with a satiny red stripe. "Mabel, we're off to have a look around."

She nodded, shrinking further, her gray robe turning to black. By the time she was done, she looked like a demon, slightly shorter than me, though with the physique of a Guard. It seemed, even disguised, she had trouble hiding her bulk. "Will this do?"

"Perfect," I said, grinning though this was deadly serious.

"Even more perfect," Sequoia said as she released Sassafras, handing him a robe. "Elph and I overheard some of the Planeless recruiting in the library. We know—or he does—where tonight's meeting is to be held."

Elph bobbed his head, drawing his hood over his horns. "It's just outside the city," he said. "If we're swift and careful, we can make it there in under an hour."

"Just in time to discover Xeoniteridone's actual agenda, I hope." I flipped up my own hood and pointed toward the door. "Lead the way."

chapter twenty seven

Our trip through Bilhaeder took about as long as Elph suggested, though it seemed we had only just reached the street when the edge of the city appeared ahead. I suppose my lack of freedom in the last four years made such an outing so enticing I barely realized the time passed.

Sneaking out of the main government building had been simple enough, with Elph to guide us around the most used areas and through little-occupied quarters. A private elevator platform in the back of the building gave us easy access to the street and our goal.

I slipped among the shadows with my head down, keeping close to Sassafras, feeling Mabel following behind me. There was every reason for me to be nervous about this plan. After all, as Ahbi continued to tell me, we had no idea if we could trust Elph. And heading out into the unknown, putting my people at risk over something that none of us understood was foolhardy. Especially since we'd seen Xeoniteridone's ability in action already. But I had to do something and the direct approach, selfish or not, was the only thing I hadn't tried.

Hands on, Ahbi sent. *What a novelty.*

Been a long time, I sent as we exited the last line of buildings and crossed into the more open area on the other side. Most demon cities didn't have suburbs. The towering domes pretty much ending abruptly, surrounded by either farmland or desert, depending on the plane in which they were originally based. Bilhaeder was no exception, and I suddenly felt exposed as Elph led us, no longer alone, down a cobbled path that led under a stone bridge. I glanced at the others making this pilgrimage in the darkness, when only a few of the moons were out, grateful for the anonymity the cloak's hood provided. I briefly considered disguising my face as well. But I had no intention of being discovered and doing so would put strain on the transformation I created for Sassafras.

I would just have to trust no one would notice one more follower in a crowd of eager Planeless.

We passed under the bridge and over a small hill, looking down into a carefully shaped valley. It had to be demon made, a type of outdoor theatre, with tiers of seating carved into the stone though no one sat. The mass of demons I'd seen at the transport platform were only a fraction of the membership milling about below. The front line stood still, facing front, while the rest moved about as though not sure what to expect.

Converts in the forefront, Mabel sent. *And newcomers in the back.*

I nodded, agreeing with her assessment. Together with a small group of demons who came up behind us, my friends and I descended into the crowd and did our best to hide among them.

Sassafras's hand brushed mine, the soft touch of fur escaping the magic holding him in demon shape. *Nectar*, he sent.

Large flasks of it were being passed around, demons imbibing with great enthusiasm. I slipped past a trio of females sharing from a silver cup while a tall demon who looked suspiciously like a Guard filled it for them.

At least we have our own confirmation of the nectar's participation in this, I sent. A tall, smiling demon stopped in my path, handing me a flask of nectar.

"Drink, sister," he said, voice almost sing-song. "Drink of the peace of the Planeless."

I hoisted the flask and pretended to drink, wiping my mouth with the back of my hand as I passed it to Sassafras. He repeated my performance before handing it to me again, lighter than it had been before.

You didn't drink it? I'm sure my eyes were huge as I realized why the flask seemed less substantial.

Of course not, he sent. *The ground at my feet is rather muddy, though.*

Clever cat, I sent. My entire body shivered just from the tiny bit of nectar touching my skin when I lifted the flask again.

"When will the festivities start?" Sass's smooth voice distracted the convert who waited for me to finish drinking. I quickly dumped the bottle to the side, turning my body so he wouldn't see as he smiled at Sass.

"Any time now," he said, voice warm with enthusiasm.

I righted the flask and finally gave it back to the happy demon with a beaming grin of my own.

"Delicious," I said.

"More awaits you," he said, gesturing me on. "The voice of our movement speaks soon. You will want to listen carefully."

"I have had the benefit of his knowledge already," I said, pretending awe and wonder. "I can't wait."

He bobbed his head before drifting on.

"Creepy," Sequoia whispered.

She could say that again.

So his power has to be tied to the nectar, Sassafras sent as we continued our press forward. He scooped a fresh flask from a passing Planeless and tucked it under his robe. *Father will want to have a look, I'm assuming.*

Smart thinking. I nodded to him before turning my

attention back to the crowd. I was tall, and able to see over most of the heads in the crowd, but as we came closer to the middle, I felt the press of demons around me and suddenly felt very small indeed.

Just as we reached the back of the line of the faithful, the crowd broke into a hearty cheer. I stopped my forward motion and looked up at the stage set at the end of the theater. Xeoniteridone had emerged from wherever he'd been hiding, and, to my horror, Ram stood at his right side, the other two demons I saw at the transport platform with the Planeless leader as well.

He has a position of privilege, Sequoia sent.

Either Xeoniteridone is aware of your relationship with Ram, Sass sent, *which is likely, and he wishes to use Ram against you, or he sees something in the young demon that interests him.*

Possibly a combination of both, Mabel sent. *Regardless, he is unreachable at this time.*

I wondered then where Bakari had gone and if I'd put him in more danger than necessary. Looking at Ram, seeing how he genuflected to Xeoniteridone and feeling nothing from him, I knew he was well and truly lost to me.

Was he even in there anymore, the Ram I knew? I turned away, catching Elph's eyes as he reached out and squeezed my hand.

Comforted by his touch, I squeezed back as Xeoniteridone began to speak.

He raised his arms to shoulder height, spark flaring to life on the tip of his staff, casting cold, white light over the front ranks of the faithful. The cult leader seemed to glow, taking on a phosphorescence that lit him like the angel he appeared to be.

"My children," he said, voice carrying, supported by demon magic. The emptiness, the cloud of nothing, formed above us again, in greater strength than before. It settled quickly, washing down over me though I was unaffected, a bubbling darkness waking a moment, as it had when I'd first met the Planeless leader, before dying off again. I felt Sassafras tense next to me, heard Sequoia's soft gasp and knew, if either of them had ingested the nectar, they would be as lost as Ram. As it was, they swayed and held on to my mind as Ahbi and I, backed by Mabel, offered them power to lean on. "You are all welcome into the ranks of the Planeless."

The entire group of demons swayed in answer.

Remarkable, the drach sent. She felt unfazed by the contact.

Is it influencing you? What did she have that made her immune? And, for that matter, what did I have? Was it simply I'd seen past him the first time? It couldn't be that simple.

Not in the least, she sent. *But I can feel it attempting to reach me. Most ingenious. And terrible.* She turned her head, sparkling diamonds behind amber eyes. *The worst kind of enslavement, Ruler. That of the heart.*

I looked back as Xeoniteridone went on.

"Our number grows," he said, the emptiness thickening and winding through the gathering, pooling only to rise again in soft waves of whispering joy and love. All false, all smoke and mirrors. "With every day, the promise of peace and freedom for our people grows with us."

Syd. Sassafras's mental voice came across crisp and afraid. *We have to contact Syd right now. This is far worse than I expected.*

Agreed, Mabel sent. *With power like this, Xeon could conceivably take over the entirety of Demonicon in a few short months.*

Weeks, Ahbi sent. Her fear was the worst of all because it matched and fed mine. *Meira, we have to do something.*

Not here, and not now. Sassafras latched onto my mind. *We have to get out of here.*

We can't. I held them all in place as the crowd swayed to something Xeoniteridone said. I no longer paid attention to his words. I'd heard and seen enough. *If we try to leave now, they will know we're not one of them.* I let them all feel my anger, bubbling to the surface to burn through my fear. *But I will see this ended,* I sent. *I will shut him down personally, and to hell with the politics of it. I'd rather go to the volcano stripped of power and position than allow this false prophet to ruin Demonicon.*

It won't come to that, Mabel sent. *The drach will never let you be punished for this.*

Comforting to know she and her people were behind me.

For now, I sent, *hold on as best you can and wait until this is over. Then I'm going home to gather my army and crush this movement before it spreads any further.*

As I turned to meet Mabel's eyes, mine settled on a familiar face staring right at me.

With an evil smile, Tanasharia swept back her hood and pointed at me, her voice cutting the night air, words carrying on her own power as she screeched her message.

"Ruler has come!" She turned to meet Xeoniteridone's eyes, her triumph so powerful I almost missed the fact she still had access to her magic where the rest of the crowd felt as powerless as Ram. "My lord, she is among us!"

chapter twenty eight

Xeon's reaction wasn't what I expected. Though the crowd around me spun to stare and glare while Tanasharia and her posse of cronies faced me down, the Planeless leader smiled with his benevolence, waving me forward.

"Allow her to pass, my children," he said. "Let Senne Hathenemeria join us in celebrating the freedom of our people."

We could fight our way out. Sassafras's nervousness wasn't making things any easier.

No, I sent. *Let's see what Xeon has in mind. If worse comes to worse, I can call Syd.*

Maybe we should anyway, Sass sent. *She and Max appearing overhead might create enough stir we can escape.*

I strode up the path opening in the wall of demons, calling out to my sister. Of course she would be out of reach, wouldn't she? I shook my head at Sassafras who scowled back. The followers of Xeoniteridone turned to face me, eyes locked on me as I proceeded with as much confidence as I could muster. By the time I reached the edge of the stage, my friends trailing behind me, I felt myself bending under the immense pressure of all that attention.

They may have been powerless, but their mass disgust was overwhelming.

I rejected the offered hand of help from one of Xeon's acolytes and joined him on the stage. Refusing to face the crowd seemed to stir their anger further, but I wasn't here for them. Xeoniteridone's pale eyes sparkled in the light of his staff as he welcomed me with a subtle gesture.

"You have come to join the Planeless, Senne," he said.

Weight pressed into my mind, pushing down on my heart, before slipping away to the sigh of darkness as though unable to catch hold. He scowled at me, the briefest of scowls, and I knew then his failure wasn't part of his plan.

He intended to convert us, Ahbi sent. *Hope he likes surprises.*

"I have not," I said, voice boosted with power, thickening and filling it out with echoes and the reverb Ahbi used when she was Ruler. I turned at last to face the watching crowd. "I am Ruler," I said, growing in height and breadth, allowing myself to stretch and grow to three times my normal size. I towered over them, the fire of Demonicon flaming around me as I raised one arm and crushed them all with my magic. "And I order you to reject this false prophet."

Xeoniteridone's laughter was echoed by the crowd as my power slipped around them but didn't make contact. His magic might have failed with me, but mine was as much a failure. Not that I expected it to work.

We had to try, Ahbi sent.

"We are no longer yours to command," Xeoniteridone sent, rising to greet me, his form growing until we were perfectly matched. "If you are not with us, Senne, you are against us."

"Another threat," I said.

"Not at all." He shrank again, turning to the crowd. "But we will not be swayed from our path of peace."

Now it's time to get out of here, Sassafras sent as the crowd's mood shifted back to happy. *Before he suggests they tear us apart for being unbelievers.*

As much as I hate to consider using our military against these demons, Ahbi sent while I, too, returned to normal size, *we have no choice.*

I turned deliberately from Xeon and faced Ram who stood only a few feet away, watching me with contempt and sorrow.

"You must stop fighting the change, Meira," he said.

"Never." I reached out to him with one hand, knowing it showed weakness. But being so close to him again, seeing him, knowing he was lost to me made me desperate. "Ram, come with me. We will find a way to fix this."

He shook his head almost violently, backing away. "There is nothing to fix," he said, disdain and horror in his eyes. "There is nothing wrong with me. I have found my purpose, can't you see that? And you would find yours, too, if only you would join us." Ram hesitated, smiled a little. "Please, join me."

My heart snapped in that instant, Ram's sweet request bitter because I knew it wasn't him speaking. Not when Xeoniteridone controlled his soul.

I backed away, glared at the Planeless leader. "I'm leaving now," I said. "Will you try to stop me?"

He spread his hands wide. "Not at all," he said. "You are free to go. But you are not free, Senne. Not really. Until you accept the peace that true freedom brings."

Let's. Go. Sassafras's voice snapped in my head. *Now.*

I was certain they wouldn't let us leave, that I'd be walking away one moment and fighting for my life the next. Visions of Xeoniteridone pinning me to the ground and having his people force-feed me nectar made me stumble once, part way through the crowd.

"Senne," his voice reached me as I retreated, hating the taste of defeat, "I will see you soon."

We broke through the last of the converts and climbed the hill even as the crowd behind us roared their loyalty to a false prophet.

I didn't bother going back to my assigned penthouse suite, instead heading right for my transport. It would take me a few hours to return to Ostrogotho, who knew how long to gather my army…

This could take forever, I fretted to Ahbi.

"Meira." Henemordonin stormed from the domed building with the governor groveling at his side, intercepting me as I stomped up the stairs to the landing pad.

I paused long enough to glare at him before continuing my forward and upward journey, shocked to feel his hand on my arm, if only briefly. The moment Henemordonin grabbed me, Mabel acted, her power pushing him so hard he spun backward and sideways, sliding down two steps before catching himself. When he rose to his feet, he roared.

"YOU DARE!" Fire crackled around him.

"SHE DOES!" I hit him with all the power of Demonicon, though this time I didn't pin him as I had in Milanseme. I let him keep his dignity. "You are the one who is over the line, Second Seat. You will submit to your Ruler and discard your arrogance for once in your pathetic life."

I should have known, Ahbi grinned inside me. *You're a Hayle. Protecting others is your strength trigger. We could have used this ages ago.*

I didn't respond, though her revelation made me pause, as my grandfather snarled at me, more animal than demon, before catching himself and returning to his shield of pride and disapproval. "Your foolishness puts our plane at risk."

"Your attitude is interfering." I let him feel my contempt. "I'm taking my power back," I said. "And my plane. The Planeless have subjugated their last followers."

"The Planeless," he boomed, "are not our biggest problem. You are."

Son of a rot-crotched sand rat, Ahbi snarled.

"Your lack of diplomacy and heavy handed power mongering has pushed our court to the brink of falling to pieces." He was not going to blame all of this on me, even as the family, only slightly thinned by the lure of the Planeless, gathered to listen. "When not petulant and childish, refusing to work within the law, you are arrogant and prideful. Your position is no longer one of ultimate domination, no matter what your grandmother's spirit might tell you." He turned his back on me, faced the court. "It is my intention to call out Senne Hathenemeria and have her declared unfit for First Seat."

Ignore him, Ahbi sent. *Let's go.*

I can't ignore him, Grandmother. It was difficult not to

shake her, the power of Demonicon swirling in agitated fury along with her anger. "Henemordonin," I snarled. "Are you challenging your Ruler?"

He didn't turn, back still facing me, focus on the family. "Challenge is unnecessary," he said, "if the majority agrees to have her removed. We all know she was the wrong choice from the beginning. I was the first to give her the chance to prove herself, because of her bloodline." So many lies in so few words. "But she has proven herself willful, temperamental and not worthy of the throne. With each act outside the law—including confronting and threatening a group of peaceful worshipers who are trying to make a better life for themselves and all demons—she has shown her dictator's heart is alive and well."

Stop him, Sassafras sent. *Stop him now.*

But Henemordonin had their attention. "Senne Hathenemeria would see all new laws reversed and plunge us back into an age of blindness, leading us away from our current state of enlightenment."

"You're such a bastard," I snarled, mind churning as I struggled for something to say. "You know very well I've done nothing to bring harm to our people, nor would I ever."

He turned to face me at last. "Tell me, Ruler," he used the title with heavy sarcasm, "where were you going before I stopped you?"

Meira. Ahbi's mental voice was quiet and careful. *You have to stop him.*

Dad took that ability away from me a long time ago, I said, feeling my defeat grow with the disdain and hatred of the family. They had lost none of their need to depose me. In fact, as they watched, I felt their desire to see me dead grow so powerful I almost stepped back.

Lie, Ahbi sent.

"I return to Ostrogotho," I said, ignoring her and Sass's hissing in my head, "to gather my army and stop the Planeless from destroying Demonicon."

"You are the destroyer." Henemordonin jabbed a finger at me while the family's power backed him up.

"I am not." *Hold on*, I sent to Ahbi.

And opened my power to the family.

It was risky, very risky. Leaving myself bare to them meant being open to attack. But I needed them to see and feel what I knew. And the only way I could do that and have them trust me was to show them everything.

They gasped over my discoveries, shuddered at the understanding of what Xeoniteridone offered. And, en masse, they pulled their support from Henemordonin while he glowered at me with fury in his every cell.

You took a great chance, Ahbi sent. *But this is an act he would never expect and thus would never think to counter. Well done.*

"Now," I said, closing up my personal protections as

Ahbi shuddered, "my court, I go to gather our forces and fight this menace. Do I have your blessing?"

They sent it in a wave at once, for the first time their animosity toward me tempered by fear of something greater than their need for power.

I spun on my grandfather, shivering inside at how close I'd come to losing everything, and slapped him with magic. Just a sharp but subtle blow, rocking his head to one side.

"I have told you twice now, if you oppose me again," I said, knowing now I did it publicly I would be held to my word, "I will have you removed from Second Seat. Consider yourself on notice from this moment on. And should I hear of you speaking in support of the Planeless or find you've offered them any assistance in their vile takeover of our people, I will personally strip you of your power and toss you to the volcano."

I didn't wait for his response. I had the backing of the court, now, and there was nothing he could do to stop me.

chapter twenty nine

"That could have been all kinds of bad," Sassafras said as we soared in a small transport toward Ostrogotho. I appropriated a six-seater, pouring on the speed and covering the distance it took our convoy to travel in half a day to an hour. The lights of the Seat sparkled on the horizon as I answered.

"Could doesn't count," I said, reaching for Jabuticabron the moment we passed over the edge of the plane border. He answered instantly and didn't overreact when I told him what we'd discovered. Instead, in true Jabut fashion, he mentally saluted me.

I shall assemble a force at once, Ruler.

I didn't chastise him for cutting me off. He had work to do.

Instead, I sat back and rubbed the tension from my temples with my fingertips while Sassafras, now in cat form again, glared at me from his perch on my lap.

"You realize, if you fail, you've given Henemordonin a doorway into having you removed." His flat voice matched his stare. "They are with you now, but only because you have frightened them into it. If you do not shut down the Planeless, they will see your weakness and turn to Henemordonin. You know it's true, no matter what the consequences."

"I do know," I said. "Please stop preaching the obvious to me. It's not helping, Sass."

"Demon politics confuse me," Mabel said. "They know the Planeless are dangerous and yet they would side with Henemordonin and his position on the cult if Meira fails?"

"If their more powerful leader can't succeed," Sass said, "they will see the Planeless and Henemordonin as the power to support. Not logical in the least. But no one has ever accused demons of their brilliance when it comes to power."

"They will have no choice," Sequoia said in a much softer tone, stroking her brother's fur from where she sat next to me. "If the magic of Demonicon cannot win against the Planeless, they will see it as a sign this cult is the more stable power and back it, despite the consequences to their own positions." She sighed and let her hands fall back to her lap. "It is the way of demons and always has been."

"Then we don't fail," I said. "It's that simple." I reached out for Syd, feeling nothing here on Demonicon before turning to Mabel. "Where's my sister?"

She shook her head. "I do not know," she said. "Only that she and my leader are investigating."

"It would be nice to have her and Max at our side," I said as the transport soared over the city and toward the Seat. "But we can make it work without her."

When I stepped off the edge of the transport and into my quarters, Jabut was there waiting for me.

"My Ruler," he saluted physically this time. "Your army assembles."

"How long?" I strode past him on the way to the door, my friends following me as I strode the hall to the far end and pressed the stone next to the doors to my office. A small chamber opened to me, the lift inside big enough for all of us.

"A few hours," Jabut said and smiled at my wide eyes. "I've been preparing since you left, Ruler."

"Of course you have," I grinned at him. "Well done, my friend."

The elevator ejected us into a large, round laboratory where Theridialis hunkered over a long table filled with devices and glass vials. He looked up as we entered, frowning, where once he always smiled upon seeing me.

"My dear," he said. "It's terrible."

"It is." I came to a halt next to him. "But I'm

assuming you're talking about something other than what I'm talking about."

He pointed at a sheet of parchment before him, amber fire etching words on its surface. "This nectar," he said, almost spitting in fury, "is vile, disgusting… it suppresses the will of the drinker and opens their heart to whomever will fill their need. Literally creating adoration and supplication, searching for a specific power on which to attach."

"Let me guess," I said. "Sorcery."

He bobbed a nod, relief on his face though I wasn't sure how relieved he should feel. "Where this sorcery comes from, I don't know," he said. "But I will continue my research."

I turned to Sequoia who handed me the flask from the meeting, tossing it to the table at Theridialis's side. "The full-blown version," I said. "It might offer more insights. For now, I need an antidote."

He shook his head. "I'm afraid I can't offer one," he said, eager hands scooping up the flask. "Not entirely. You must find a way to counter the magic tied to the nectar. Apart, they are worthless. Together, a formidable foe."

"Can you come up with some means to stifle the effects long enough to break the sorcery's hold?" There had to be a way to free the demons in thrall of the Planeless.

"Perhaps," he said. "Used in conjunction, we may be able to shatter the connection."

It was nice to see hope on his face. "Do it," I said. "For now, we'll have to act without."

"What do you plan to do?" Theridialis looked around, meeting our faces.

"My army will put an end to their spread," I said. "I hope."

"You run a great risk," Theridialis said. "You must keep your Guard from coming in contact with the nectar and with the sorcery that triggers it. If they fall under the spell of this combination, you will be fighting your own people."

I knew that already. What was with everyone repeating the obvious?

Less than two hours later, I stood at the prow of a massive transport, dressed in heavy black armor I'd never had to don, refusing to consider I'd made a terrible mistake in confronting the Planeless head-on.

All the power of Demonicon was backed by the magic of the drach as Mabel assisted me in hurtling my forces toward Bilhaeder. The first sun was threatening to rise as we approached the city, circling toward the amphitheater and the gathered Planeless.

Still no word from Syd, I sent to Mabel.

We shall have to proceed without her, she sent.

I grunted, feeling oddly fake inside my armor as

though I played a game for which I was unprepared. But there was no time to back down now, not when the three troop transports settled to the grass surrounding the valley, the five thousand soldiers Jabuticabron was able to muster surrounding the equal number of Planeless looking up at us with defiance.

Xeoniteridone stood where I'd left him, in the center of the stage. As I stepped from the transport, my power snapping a shield around the space to contain the cult, he spoke.

"We are peaceful followers of the way of the Planeless," he said. "We offer no resistance."

"I told you once to disperse," I said, voice carrying as it had before, with the power of our plane to fill it with strength. "You declined, forcing me to bring my army to ensure the order is followed."

He lowered his arms. "You would really attack helpless and pacifist demons?"

Careful, Ahbi sent.

"Disperse," I roared. "And there will be no conflict."

My guards came to attention, their power gathering to do my bidding.

Xeoniteridone backed up a step, the Planeless swaying as he did. "I have my answer, then," he said as he addressed his followers. "We have her answer. They will never allow us to exist peacefully. And so, we must obey."

I think my jaw hit my chest, I was so shocked. The

gathered demons groaned even as Xeoniteridone gestured toward them. Power crackled and, in an instant and a rush of air, they vanished.

Gone, all five thousand of them, leaving the amphitheater completely empty. All but for Xeoniteridone who remained on the stage, facing me with his kindly smile.

They were never here. Ahbi swore softly. *He sent them elsewhere, knowing we would come. He's played us, Meira.*

"I knew you would never understand," Xeoniteridone said. "My people only want peace, and we have left peacefully." He took one further step back while bile writhed in my stomach. "But hear me, Senne. No matter what you want, peace will not be so easily silenced."

Henemordonin appeared through the ranks of soldiers and I knew then he had been watching since our arrival. "Not all of us are opposed to peace," he said.

The slimy, one-toed sloth-grub, Ahbi sent.

Xeoniteridone bowed toward him. "Then, perhaps one day, Demonicon will be ready for our way of being. Until then, I bid you farewell, Senne Hathenemeria, and I wish you joy."

He disappeared as his followers disappeared while I fumed over the futility of what I'd just experienced. No one to arrest, my army waiting for me to act.

This is a disaster, Ahbi sent. *But not a failure.*

I glared at Henemordonin. "From this moment forth,

the Planeless are banned from gathering in groups larger than a half dozen. Anyone caught doing so will be arrested and their power removed."

He didn't comment as the gathered court listened.

"And the cult leader, Xeoniteridone, is now a fugitive, wanted by the Seat." I turned to Jabut who saluted. "Dispense my armed forces to all the cities of Demonicon. Enforce my order."

"As you command, my Ruler," he boomed before spinning on his troops. "Guards of the Seat—fall in for assignments."

I left him to sort things out, knowing a huge battle of a more intimate nature was on my plate when Henemordonin stomped his way to my side and did his favorite glare down his nose at me.

"You may have managed to avoid it this time," he snarled, "but know this—I am watching you and the moment you misstep, I will ensure you never sit on First Seat again."

I let him march off with his self-righteous attitude wrapped around him even as I reached out to Jabuticabron.

I want to know where he's going, I sent. *And who he talks to.*

Jabut didn't respond with words, just a feeling of satisfaction.

You think Sassafras is right, Abhi sent. *That Henemordonin is working with the Planeless.*

I have no proof, I sent. *But it's a very real possibility. And even if he isn't, I can't allow him to put all of Demonicon at risk.* I drew a long breath before returning to the transport. *We may have to kill him after all.*

chapter thirty

I settled behind my desk with a pounding headache and no desire to tackle the stack of paperwork awaiting my attention. It had been three days since our return to Ostrogotho, three days since Xeoniteridone and the Planeless vanished from sight. There had been no further instances of their appearing, all quiet around Demonicon, according to Jabuticabron. And no further outflux of demons from the cities or loss of soldiers to them, so I could only believe Xeoniteridone was good to his word.

For now, that was. I had little doubt he was scheming something different now that I'd curtailed his overt activities.

One good thing came from this—Zinniaperimote's warning about Tanasharia, and my cousin's plan to challenge me for the throne was obviously no longer an option. The young demon was gone with the Planeless.

The air beside me shimmered and the veil parted, my sister stepping through. I rose to greet her, hugging Syd before she pushed me back with a worried frown.

"This sucks," she said. "I'm sorry I was gone so long. Are you okay?"

"I could ask the same about you," I said, sitting on the edge of my desk as she began her typical pacing. "What happened?"

"This whole damage to the veil thing isn't a little problem," she said before coming to a halt and slapping both fists against her thighs. "Meems, when I think about what Gabriel's power did in under a minute..." She shuddered. "Max and the drach have their hands full."

"So you've been helping them?" A tiny thread of resentment died as I crushed it under my newfound confidence. Yes, I'd failed in a way. But I no longer feared my grandfather and, as a happy side effect of the last week or so, the attitude of my family had altered to grudging respect. It wasn't much, considering Xeoniteridone was still out there, but I'd accept it with gratitude and move on.

"Not exactly." Her beautiful face twisted in irritation. "I've been arguing with the maji."

"Ah," I said. "A lesson in futility?"

"You can say that again," she said. "Idiots. They refuse to lift a freaking finger to heal the veil, like it's got nothing to do with them or something stupid." She chewed her bottom lip. "Arrogant asses. And Fate was equally useless."

The two halves of Fate, female and male, never seemed to come up with much we could use. "What about the dark maji?"

"Can you say annoying?" Syd tossed her hands in the air. "I might as well be beating my damned head against a brick wall. Craptastically frustrating." She grunted before shrugging. I know it wasn't funny, but I grinned as she rolled her eyes at me. "Smartass," she said.

"Well, I hate to add to your worry," I said. "But what do we do about Demonicon's sorcery problem?" I was no longer above asking her for help. It had been proven very clearly to me in the near past, taking back control of Demonicon fully would be a group effort.

Syd tensed, face darkening.

"I had no idea," she said, tension remaining so coiled I feared she might crack. "I'll add it to the list. But the Brotherhood... Meems, there must be another answer. We've been watching closely—both the Councils and the Steam Union—but Liander Belaisle and his pack of nasty haven't made a peep."

"And if this is an old setup, one Belaisle established before you kicked his ass?" I thought of the fallen Brotherhood leader, his smarmy smile, his arrogance, and how he always seemed to be three or four steps ahead of Syd no matter what she did.

Syd sighed. "I guess it's possible," she said. "I'll keep looking into it." She tried to smile, eyes sparking with anger I knew wasn't aimed at me. "Anything else?"

"That's it," I said. "Is there anything *I* can do to help *you?*"

She shook her head, ponytail bouncing over her t-shirt shoulder, anxiety leaving her. I didn't think my sister would ever change. At least, I hoped not. I loved her casual confidence so much, the way she absorbed and then shook off trouble. It took a great deal of effort not to leap up and hug her again.

"We'll work it out," she said. "I may have to conduct an in-depth hunt for Brotherhood stench while unblocking Gabriel's ability to make Gates and see if he can fix the veil." Syd laughed. "Like a five year old boy with the soul of a Fey is capable of repairing the entire veil between Universes." She winked. "Totally plausible."

"He's your son," I said. "Wouldn't surprise me in the least." I ducked my head when I asked the question weighing on my mind. "Is it all right if I keep Sass for a while?" It was selfish of me, but I'd grown to love having him with me again. Despite what he said about their protection being handled by others, I knew Sass's main calling was protecting young Hayle witches.

Syd shrugged with a grin. "He's a free cat," she said. She came to me and hugged me, kissing my cheek. "Got to run," she said. "And see if my kid can actually pull this off." She let me go, retreating to the fresh tear in the veil. "Keep me posted?"

"You, too." I waved as she left, wondering what I would ever do without her.

The door to my office opened, Elph's handsome face peeking through. He'd stood at my side the entire ordeal and, in the last three days, made himself an invaluable part of my team. I waved him inside, settling in my chair again as he approached with an armload of fresh parchment. I groaned at the sight, to which he laughed.

"My Ruler," he said, setting them before me, "I'm sorry, but it's necessary."

"I know," I said, rolling my shoulders under the tension of knowing I had a long night ahead of me. "I can take it."

He slipped around behind me, hands sliding down my neck, fingers firmly massaging the tight muscles. I relaxed into his touch, closing my eyes, enjoying the pressure of his hands and the gentle caress of his power. My eyes flew open as he bent and softly kissed my cheek. I turned to face him, the press of his lips on mine ever-so-tender.

"I'll bring you dinner in a little while," he whispered before leaving me to work.

My fingers lingered over the place his lips had lain, tracing the path from my cheekbone to my mouth. Though I didn't exactly want him to stop his advances, my worry for Ram was still in the forefront of my mind.

Theridialis insisted there was a way, after all, to break the hold of the nectar, now that he had access to the full-strength version, which gave me great hope.

We just had to find Ram, kidnap him, snap the sorcery holding him and find a cure for the nectar. Small beans.

Thinking of Ram made me ponder Bakari. He'd appeared to me after Henemordonin returned the day after I did. The assassin promised he and his people were searching for the Planeless, but they were as vulnerable to the cult as anyone.

I settled in to do my duty as Ruler as night fell over my world and I did my best to convince myself I may have lost a few battles, but I'd win the war if it killed me.

Like what you read? Find out more at
pattilarsen.com

Here's a look at the first chapter of
Book Two of the First Plane Trilogy

chapter one

The droning sound of my grandfather's voice was the last thing I wanted to listen to this morning. I'd been hearing far too much from him in the past week, something I was quick to realize wasn't about to go away any time soon.

Lies, all of it. My demon grandmother groused in my head, her spirit thrashing in fury as Henemordonin, Second Seat of Demonicon, expounded to the court how sunny and shiny and full of butterflies and sparkles our plane was. Despite the fact my forces were still at large, patrolling the cities and settlements, searching for the Planeless, a cult preaching peace and light to all demons, my grandfather assured the gathered royal family everything was hunky dory.

They don't care, I sent to Ahbi as Henemordonin went on, blocking out his speech, more of the same from yesterday and the day before that and the day before that. *All they want is for things to work in their favor. And if that requires sticking their heads in the sand, they'll do it and be happy for it.*

If only there was something I could do. I'd made illegal the meetings of the cult, set my finest scientist on the task of finding an antidote for the nectar the Planeless used to sway the hearts and minds of the demons they recruited and ordered the leader of the sect, Xeoniteridone, arrested. All without a scrap of support from my Second Seat.

We already know he's up to something, Ahbi sent as Henemordonin's voice dropped. I'd begun to notice, now I paid attention to his tactics instead of his bullying, he had a rhythm to his delivery. He always began his presentations with a dire forecast, spinning out the negatives should anyone within hearing range go against him, then leading them into his way of thinking before offering a dire warning if they failed and finally wrapping up with a positive message to reinforce the notion they needed to trust him and only him.

He learned that from me, Ahbi sent. *Though I gave up using it centuries ago. Got boring.*

I almost laughed. Except our present situation was far from funny. Bad enough my father and former Ruler, Haralthazar, started his demonocracy campaign before I took the throne. But his lack of follow through left me hanging, scrambling to regain the power he gave away. I spent four years suffering the effects of his decisions, four years under my grandfather's thumb. Four years in which my power was removed further and further from me.

Standing up to him helped. Ahbi shifted restlessly inside me as we both felt the family sway once again to Henemordonin's side. I didn't bother considering a rebuttal. It never did me a scrap of good to fight with him publicly.

Not exactly true, Ahbi sent. *You certainly put him in his place when we confronted the Planeless.* She had it right, and I couldn't have been happier to show my grandfather he couldn't just set me aside and pat my head like a nice little demon. I might have only been eighteen, but I sat in Ruler's seat, not him. And when the Planeless openly and brazenly recruited a massive number of demons from under my nose, I had to act. It still made me anxiously curious why Henemordonin stood against my choice to bring in the army, though I couldn't bring myself to believe he had anything to do with the cult.

I have to agree, Ahbi sent. *He's too in love with his own power to side with a sect that suppressed the magic of demons. He'd never allow his own to be subjugated.*

We still have no idea what Xeoniteridone's ultimate plan is, I sent. *And where his sorcery came from.* That was a massive shock, discovering a demon who had sorcery. According to everyone I knew, it was simply impossible. Demons didn't have the dark, devouring power, fed by the element of fire instead.

We'll find out, Ahbi sent. *Just as soon as we do something permanent to your grandfather.*

I still shuddered from the idea of having him removed so blatantly. *I know it would make things easier if he were to have an accident*, I sent. *But if we make the attempt and it fails, you know it's going to come back on us.*

It won't fail, she growled. *Sick Mabel on him.*

I did grin this time, squashing my expression quickly. Lucky enough, no one was looking at me and so they missed my amusement. *I only wish*, I sent, thinking of the drach female I'd just started to get to know. *She's gone back with the rest of her people, remember?* Mabel had a distinct dislike for my grandfather and already offered to eat him despite her revulsion at the idea. I would have settled for char broiled.

We could call her back, Ahbi sent. *I'm sure she'd do it as a favor to you. She likes you.*

I like her, too, I sent. *But the drach are too busy.* The second surprise came, not only for me, but my sister, Sydlynn Hayle, the leader of the Hayle coven back home and new maji who risked everything to save the Universe, including the people she loved. I wished she was here right now, even as I straightened on my throne and reminded myself I was Ruler and didn't need my crazy talented sister to rescue me. Besides, she was off with

Max, the leader of the drach, and the rest of the first race, trying to heal the damage Syd's son, Gabriel, did to the veil when he was forced to open a Gateway to the other Universe.

I perked as Henemordonin's voice climbed the register, out of the doldrums and into a more normal, brighter tone. "And I can assure you, with the utmost in confidence," he smiled, and I swear I caught a sparkle in his eye as he gestured with grand arrogance, "our people, our planes, are safe and secure under my rule."

Oh, he so did not just say that out loud, Ahbi snarled.

I sighed in my head, holding very still as he turned slowly and with absolute deliberation, toward me, still smiling.

"Very well," I said in as bored a tone as I could wrangle while my grandmother raged in my head. "Thank you for your little update, Henemordonin. Was there anything else?"

His jaw jumped. It was oh-so-very hard not to grin in his face. While I had become fearful of him yelling at me, enduring so much abuse I retreated from it, I'd come to find my strength again and, in doing so, took great pleasure in undercutting him in the subtlest ways. I could see why Ahbi loved being Ruler so much in these moments.

My grandfather didn't comment as all the work he'd put into his speech unraveled in a tittering wave of amusement from the court.

Ahbi's anger stilled. *Sizzle*, she sent.

Not done, I sent. "I do hope not," I said, looking away from him with a slow eye roll. "We have more important matters to deal with than yet another long-winded explanation why you are the center of the Universe."

Meira! Ahbi gasped a laugh.

You approve? I gestured to the front of the line where the demons waiting for audience stood. As the first stepped forward, Henemordonin sank into his throne, still glaring at me.

Very well done, she sent, chuckling with evil intent. *Let him chew on that slap on the face for the next few hours.*

I'm less worried about his posturing in court, I sent as I half-listened to the whining of yet another demon noble who wanted something someone else already owned, *and more about Jabuticabron's silence.*

Ahbi's laughter fell quiet. *Agreed*, she sent. *I know Henemordonin is blocking us.*

As long as that's all it is, I sent. *And not that he's been influenced by the Planeless.*

She didn't comment as I listened to Henemordonin pronounce his decision for the demon before me. I'd taken to allowing him to run the minutia of court, though I was careful to handle the big stuff myself. Let him ponder the significance of adultery, theft and scandal. I had more important issues to deal with.

Such as the virulent plague that was the cult. We'd already lost many demons to it, the combination of the nectar and Xeoniteridone's coercive power tied to his sorcery making short work of even the most loyal demons. Among them was Rameranselot, a friend and, I hoped one day, my mate.

You're getting ahead of yourself, Ahbi sent. *He's said no in the past.*

The truth of Ram's rejection stung far more than anything Henemordonin could throw at me these days.

He'll come around, I sent. *If we can rescue him and reverse the effects of the nectar.*

He'd gone from faithful guardian/conspirator/friend to rabid follower of the Planeless in a heartbeat, at least according to my Guard captain, Jabuticabron. It still amazed me how quickly the change happened and, if I hadn't watched it with my own eyes that night in Bilhaeder, I still wouldn't believe it was possible for ordinary, power loving demons to willingly give up their magic and their passion for gathering more in exchange for peace and powerlessness.

It makes no sense, Ahbi agreed. *But it's fact.*

I reached for Jabuticabron as Henemordonin continued his Second Seat duties, dealing with the complainants before us. Almost immediately I felt the wall around him, familiar magic blocking me from reaching him.

the planeless

Just push through, Ahbi growled. *Your grandfather has earned no respect. Don't even think about taking it easy on him.*

I'd rather he didn't know I was talking with Jabuticabron, I sent. *If Henemordonin wants to hide what's happening from me, there's a good reason for it. I'll get to the bottom of it, even if I have to go through Sequoia.* My Guard captain's sister, Avenesequoia, was among my cherished friends and allies. The siblings of my darling silver Persian/demon boy, Sassafras, they had both taken it upon themselves upon my arrival on Demonicon to watch over and take care of me. I was grateful for both of them, partly because having them with me felt like Sass was at my side.

I've hardly vanished, his crisp voice broke through.

Eavesdropper, I sent. *Can you reach your brother?*

Not yet, Sass sent. *But Sequoia is on it.*

As long as you allow your grandfather to use the new laws against you, Ahbi sent, cutting Sassafras off, *he will continue to chip away at your influence until no amount of embarrassing him in front of the court will do you a bit of good. You're on your way to being a figurehead, Meira. Don't think he's not working on new laws to bring you down.*

Ruler. Sequoia's mind touched mine, hers flavored with mint and bright yellow light.

I shifted slightly in my seat as she spoke. *What is it?*

Jabuticabron is here, she sent. *But I can't reach him.* I could feel her moving rapidly, her mind anxious. *I caught sight of him being herded by his own Guards into your grandfather's office.*

The bastard. Ahbi seized control and tried to force me to my feet. I could only thank the elements for Sassafras who shoved against her so hard, his power joining mine. I soft grunt of expelled air left my lips as we pinned Ahbi together.

I really worry about you, Sass sent to her directly. *You used to be so in control, Ahbi Sanghamitra. What's become of your soul?*

I've been murdered, she snarled, *forced to live inside the Node of Demonicon and not one, but two, Hayle witches.* She almost panted her frustration. *All while the power of my position is being stripped away by a demon I should have had killed on our wedding night.*

Grandmother. I sent soothing energy as she settled, still fuming. *I'm so sorry.* There was a time when we butted heads over her need to control everything. But I'd come to feel terribly for her, empathetic she'd lost everything in her need to protect Demonicon. *It's going to be all right.*

She grumbled and turned her back on me internally, falling silent, her sullen quiet making me sigh again.

Ruler. Sequoia felt stationary now. *Did you want me to try to see Jabut?*

No. I sat up straighter on my throne. *Just keep an eye on him if you can. We'll be done here, soon and then I'll come get him personally.*

Sassafras showed me an image of himself, perched on the window seat of my quarters, his amber eyes glowing while he hopped down and sashayed his furry butt to the door.

I'm coming to meet you, he sent to Sequoia. *Meira, I'll see you there.*

Anticipation rose like a ball of fire in my stomach. Henemordonin may have cornered me, cancelled out my ability to confront him directly and done his best to remove what power I had over my people, but I'd be damned if he'd turn me into some figurehead.

about the author

Everything you need to know about me is in this one statement: I've wanted to be a writer since I was a little girl, and now I'm doing it. How cool is that, being able to follow your dream and make it reality? I've tried everything from university to college, graduating the second with a journalism diploma (I sucked at telling real stories), am part of an all-girl improv troupe (if you've never tried it, I highly recommend making things up as you go along as often as possible). I've even been in a Celtic girl band (some of our stuff is on YouTube!) and was an independent film maker. My life has been one creative thing after another—all leading me here, to writing books for a living.

Now with multiple series in happy publication, I live on beautiful and magical Prince Edward Island (I know you've heard of Anne of Green Gables) with my very patient husband and multitude of pets.

I love-love-love hearing from you! You can reach me (and I promise I'll message back) at patti@pattilarsen.com. And if you're eager for your next dose of Patti Larsen books (usually about one release a month) come join my mailing list! All the best up and coming, giveaways, contests and, of course, my observations on the world (aren't you just dying to know what I think about everything?) all in one place: http://smarturl.it/PattiLarsenEmail.

Last—but not least!—I hope you enjoyed what you read! Your happiness is my happiness. And I'd love to hear just what you thought. A review where you found this book would mean the world to me—reviews feed writers more than you will ever know. So, loved it (or not so much), **your honest review would make my day**. Thank you!